Whisterpoop

A Romantic Comedy

2021

Cover art by CozyCoverDesigns.com

First Printing: 2021

ISBN: 9798536396018

Other books by R.J. Corgan
Cold Flood
The Meerkat Murders
Murder on Masaya

Visit www.RJCorganBooks.com for more information.

Dedicated to my librarians:
Janet, Dawn, Cathy, Roxanne, and Pat

Whisterpoop - definition: (v) a small smack upside the head.

Chapter 1

Sunday evening, July 1999
109 Willow Leaf Lane

Professor Katherine Stone, looking resplendent in her scarlet dress, lowered the smoking musket even as the Archduke Delano pressed the dagger against the neck of Enrique, her lover. Stone watched dispassionately as a crimson stain spread slowly across the fabric of the Archduke's chest. Delano's eyes widened and his whole body twitched before he drew a shuddering, final breath. The blade slid through the slick leather of his glove, sparkling in the flickering torchlight as it tumbled to land with a clatter atop the cobbles.

Katherine's lips stretched into a bloodless white line as she watched Delano's body slump onto the filthy street.

Enrique broke from the grasp of his captor. He pulled her close, his strong arms pressing her bosom against his body. In that moment, he knew they would be together forever.

~ φ ~

Mrs. Karen Whittington closed the book with a sigh and placed it atop the pile that stood by her recliner. She reflected that in Katherine's time it was uncommon for people to even reach middle age. Perhaps then, she pondered, you really could live happily ever after.

Middle age.

Such a horrid term.

Probably made up by some *young* person.

Karen adjusted her reading glasses and reached for her new purchase that rested on the plush velvet armrest of her chair. With something approaching reverent awe, she picked up the crinkled paper bag and unsheathed its contents: a new Katherine Stone paperback. She slanted the cover toward the lamp and its honey-tinted glow skimmed across the slick cover of the volume, highlighting the flowing silk of the heroine's dress and emphasizing the contours of the hero's abdominals. The scent of fresh ink made her giddy with anticipation.

Karen had waited at the bookstore all afternoon for the shipment to arrive, lounging around the self-improvement section until the boxes were wheeled out from the back. She had bought the first copy and sped home, completely forgetting to purchase more cat food from the market.

After nearly a year of waiting for the next installment, and constantly badgering the bookstore owner for the publication date, she finally had the latest Katherine Stone novel in her hands. She peeled open the cover and rushed through the copyright and acknowledgement rubbish until she reached the title page:

THE ETERNAL PASSION SERIES
VOLUME VIII:
LOVE AND TREACHERY
IN THE DARKNESS OF THE SUBCONTINENT

Featuring Dr. Katherine Stone,
Famed Geographer, Adventuress, and Reckless Lover.

Karen had just finished re-reading *Eternal Passion VII, Love Under the Tuscan Moon,* to refresh her memory of how the last installment had ended. However, she reluctantly placed the book back inside its bag. *Eternal Passion VIII* must wait until after supper.

Something as precious as this must be savored, like a fine wine.

Or at least with a box of cheap Merlot.

She rose from her recliner and shuffled in her furry slippers into the dining room. Striking a match, she lit the candles on the table. Exhaling a sigh that threatened to extinguish the flames, she drew up her chair and settled her nightgown about the seat. Then she opened the box of Merlot and filled her glass from the spigot.

Karen had handled turning thirty-five all right: a quick trip to London with her husband, Michael, had served to muffle that chime of her biological clock. After the "Incident," forty had been ignored in the hopes that it would just go away—please. She had treated that birthday just like any other day, except for unplugging the phone to prevent calls from her sons. But around the forty-five-year mark, accompanied by an onslaught of arthritis, came the certainty that time was most definitely *not* going to just go away.

She looked at the turkey dinner arranged on her dining room table. The bird in its golden-basted glory lay nestled between the stuffing, mashed potatoes, gravy, and cranberry sauce—the real thing, not that God-awful canned stuff—all plated nicely in fine china dishes, bowls, and boats, all waiting to be consumed.

It was her fiftieth birthday.

Luckily, it was also a Sunday, which had allowed her to hide from the local populace of the village of Little Ivory, as well as her co-workers. She had slept in, read the Sunday comics followed by eight romance novels, and had spent the rest of the day cooking.

There was enough food for six people. It would probably last her a week.

The yellow glow of the candles lit up the dark, gloomy wood-paneled room. She stared at the three empty chairs that stood sentinel around the table. Her boys were away. Tommy was in the Corps and Jimmy, her dearest, was in the city. And as for Michael, her husband, well Michael couldn't come, because, well, he was dead.

Typical.

He was always such a difficult man.

Karen found herself staring at Michael's empty chair. She remembered a similar scene from Christmas as a child. Each year she had written to Santa, asking for Daddy to be home for Christmas dinner. Sometimes Santa and the Corps would cooperate, and her father would be there. Usually, however, he wouldn't be able to come, and Karen would be seated across from his empty chair. The next day, Santa would receive a very cross letter from little Karen Whittington that stated, very implicitly, that she no longer believed in him.

She always wrote the next year asking for the same thing, though.

She reached out for the wine glass and raised it to her lips.

And paused.

"No." She set the wine glass firmly on the table, the thump muted by the white linen. She folded her slim hands onto her lap and addressed the world at large. "This is simply too depressing. I will not have it. I will not wallow in self-pity. I will not get drunk on my birthday by myself!"

She nodded, filled with determination, but then she caught sight of her reflection on the belly of the silver gravy boat: her sandy gray hair tumbled down across her shoulders, her bosom was wrapped in the flannel of her night gown, and even in the candlelight, she could see the creases and folds that had taken up residence beneath her eyes and along the folds of her mouth. She stared into the fluttering flame of a candle, lost in a haze of times long past, when the chairs weren't empty and the room was never silent, despite her every wish at the time.

She reached for the glass again, absently, but caught herself once more.

This was not helping. She returned to the kitchen and mucked about in some of her less-used cupboards, routing through old pasta holders, punch bowls, and blenders. With a gasp of delight, she dragged a cup from the furthest reaches of the vestibule and blew off the dust of twenty years. Satisfied, she moved to the refrigerator and opened the door, wincing at the harsh white light that slapped at her eyes. Finally, she emerged into the dining room with a large margarita glass clasped in both hands, the rim encrusted with grated Parmesan flakes and the bowl filled with a white fluid. She placed the glass at the head of the table opposite her and brought out a plate on which she put a serving of turkey and gravy.

"Mr. Hobbes, dinner is served!" she called.

Receiving no response, she strode into the living room and retrieved a large furry bundle. She seated the calico cat on the chair and took her own place at the table.

Karen returned to her own chair and served herself large helpings of food.

~ φ ~

Mr. Hobbes peered over the edge of the table, eyeing his plate cautiously. His servant had been behaving very oddly of late in his opinion; he chose never to sit on the table, let alone eat meals there. It was a subject that neither he nor his servant had ever seen eye to eye on. Mr. Hobbes wasn't quite sure what to make of this latest development.

Karen raised her glass of Merlot in a toast.

4

"Technically, I still have half my life yet to live. Here's to the second half!"

Mr. Hobbes sniffed the glass of milk, licked his lips, and started in on the turkey before she could change her mind.

Chapter 2

Karen awoke sprawled across the couch, her face embedded in an empty box of cherry cordials. That damn new Japanese alarm clock Tommy had mailed her was screeching horribly away in her bedroom. She managed to pry off the sticky circular wrappers from her face and call in sick at work before passing out again.

At ten o'clock, wrapped in her bathrobe and slippers, she managed to sprint—yes, *sprint,* she was quite pleased that she could still do that at least—to retrieve the mail. Nothing but the usual junk: electricity bill, coupon book, and a packet of seeds from her gardening club.

She flopped on the couch and stared blankly at *The Price Is Right.* An extremely bloated Mr. Hobbes was lodged in a corner of the couch and absolutely refused to be moved. He was content to chase a sunbeam between naps for most of the morning before disappearing for extended periods to his cat box.

So far day one of *Life: The Sequel* was not beginning at all well. She hadn't even managed to even start reading her new novel. *Eternal Passions VIII* still lay shrouded in its wrappings, as her system had been unprepared for the triple onslaught of wine, turkey, and chocolate.

Shortly before noon, she felt sufficiently recovered to face the world. The fact that she had read all the romance novels she had checked out of the library cemented her decision. Having called in sick, it wouldn't be wise to be seen. If she was quick, however, she could nip in and top up her supply without her manager noticing. She gathered up her old books, stuffed a few string grocery bags into her pocket, and collected her checkbook and purse. Thus armed, she strode out through the front door, her thoughts bent on feline antacids.

~ φ ~

Little Ivory, it was said, was given its name by the original pioneers who found the nearly year-round blanket of snow both blissful and pure. Later travelers quickly discovered that although snow fell often enough, thanks to the plows and salt trucks, the

6

landscape persisted in a state of slushy brown for eight months of the year. While those original adventurers, and indeed most people today, passed quickly through the tiny valley village to greener fields many miles south, Karen adored it.

It was the villagers she couldn't stand.

Nestled in the valley of the St. Lawrence River, the village had escaped flood, fire, revolution, and the French. Despite any views the rest of the world might hold to the contrary, the inhabitants of Little Ivory maintained that they were British, through and through. The Victorian houses that lined the roads were a testament to this heritage, along with the twelve pubs, the village's primary source of tourism and income.

Decades of living through dark winter nights, encased in snow and frozen rain, had an odd effect on the people of Little Ivory. The residents' skin was pale and thin, and time seemed to take an exaggerated toll on the populace, aging them beyond their years.

The students at the local college maintained that was because there was simply nothing to do in the town and that the stooped shoulders of the villagers were weighed down by the crushing boredom that hung in the air throughout the season.

It was high summer now though, making the winter slush seem unimaginable as flowers bloomed and the late morning sun baked the asphalt of the road as Karen's car crept down the main road into the small village. She parked behind the Civic Center, dropped her returns in the orange book drop next to the post box, and made her way through the parking lot. For convenience the museum, town hall, library, and fire station were located in the same building. The sirens of the fire engines had yet to cause a heart attack among the library's elderly patrons, but Karen suspected it was only a matter of time. She made her way to the back door and entered the Ivory Public Library through the basement and shuffled through the dark room.

The place had a particularly musty, book-ish smell about it. *Reader's Digest*, Zane Grey, *National Geographic,* and soft-smut were stacked by the walls and slathered across dozens of fold-up tables. There were hundreds, perhaps thousands, of paperbacks that had been donated over the years for the annual book sale during the town's summer fair but never sold. Since most of the people who attended the book sale were the chief donator's, this could hardly be considered surprising.

Except perhaps, Karen smiled, to Elsa, their acquisitions librarian, who could never quite work out why, after every book sale, they had more books than they had the previous year. As Karen drifted through the room, she let her fingers brush against the bindings, their titles invisible in the gloom. She had no need of light; she had weeded out all the "quality" books when they had been donated. One of the perks of her job at the library.

She jerked her hand back with a muttered curse as an edge sliced through the skin of her index finger. She reflexively smacked the offensive book with her purse, scattering Louis L'Amours across the cement floor.

"Damn," she mumbled around her finger as she sucked on it. She bent down and gathered up the debris with her free hand, before dumping them in a random pile back on the table. As she did so, her gaze happened on a pile of vinyl LPs stacked next to the westerns. Picking up the top few, she tilted them into the faint rays of sunlight that trickled in through the basement windows so that she could read the jacket sleeves. "*Duke Ellington*," read one, "*George Gershwin*," another, and the next was "*Irving Berlin*." An idea started to form in her head, but the specifics eluded her. Sucking thoughtfully, she replaced the discs and headed to the stairs.

She slipped into the library proper through a back door marked "Private." The ruby red carpet installed in the seventies had been trodden down over the years into a dull shade of hibiscus. The white walls stretched up several stories to a balcony lined with balustrades that overlooked rows of beige metal shelving that lead to a wall filled with a giant walnut card catalogue. The front desk, a sweeping arm of oak, curled toward the main entrance, where a tall grandfather clock stood guard, its massive brass pendulum bob slowly sweeping back and forth like an all-seeing eye.

Karen made her way through the stacks toward the front desk. There lay her goal: the paperback shelves labeled "Romantic Fiction."

Thankfully, no one was browsing, so she pulled open her drawstring bag and placed it at one end of the shelf. Then, she placed her hand at the far end of the books and *pushed*. The novels

8

slid down along the metal rack and plopped, one by one, into her bag. She pulled the clasp tight and dragged the bundle to the front desk and heaved it up onto the checkout counter.

"How many will it be today, Mrs. Whittington?" Patrick asked from behind the desk.

"Thirty-two," she replied. "I think. It should hold me to Thursday at any rate."

"Thirty-two," echoed Patrick as he wrote the number down on a scrap of paper by the computer. He was a scrawny high school student with curly, black hair. His voice had only begun to change and generally wavered between a high-pitched whine and a scratchy baritone that Karen found constantly endearing. And entertaining.

"Are you all by yourself this afternoon?"

"Nah, Mrs. Carlson is in the back somewhere." He stuffed the scrap of paper under the keyboard. "She should be right back if you would like to speak with her."

"Oh?"

Patrick glanced up from the monitor screen at the tone of her voice.

Karen felt her face begin to twitch.

"Oh. Oh . . . good." She clutched her bundle against her chest. "Well, see you later, Patrick. Books to buy, shopping to read . . ." She trailed off as she made a dash for the main exit.

"Karen, darling, you do look nice today!" called a voice.

Karen let an exaggerated sigh hiss through her lips as she turned to face Mrs. Carlson. "You make that sound like a surprise," she muttered. Mrs. Carlson was the first, and only, person to bear the name Mavis that Karen had ever met. No one, in Karen's opinion, deserved it more.

"How are you feeling?" Resplendent in her purple polyester tights, Mavis' eyes glowed with curiosity.

"Pretty gassy, actually," replied Karen, "But I expect it's those sausages I had for breakfast. I'll give you a call when they've passed all the way through."

Mavis hesitated for a moment, as if not certain how to respond. Then, she barked out a short laugh and waved her hands at Karen in dismay. "Now stop that Karen, I know it must be hard, but it has to happen to all of us someday."

"Not really, no. A strict diet avoiding products wrapped with intestines should do the trick for most people."

The smile remained plastered to Mavis' face as she bravely pressed on. "Turning fifty doesn't have to be depressing, my dear. I haven't yet glided past that landmark of life—"

More likely you've tripped over it and landed face down in the mud. Karen eyed her gossip-mongering friend. Just how old are you? She looked at the bouffant perched on Mavis' head, just a little too clear of gray, and the skin around the eyes a little too tight to be convincing.

"But when I do, I'm sure I will celebrate it with a huge party!" Mavis finished.

No, you wouldn't. You'd more likely end up in a clinic. Maybe you already have . . .

Mavis obviously found Karen's silence unnerving. She fiddled with the gaudy rings that studded her pudgy fingers and continued to blather on in the hopes of eliciting a response.

"I called round yesterday to say hello, but there was no answer at the front door and the back gate was latched . . ."

That's because I saw your car pull up and grabbed Mr. Hobbes and we hid in the kitchen until you had gone.

"I was probably out for a walk, taking in nature's splendor," Karen finally replied. "I tend to do that to celebrate tragic moments."

"We must have a party!" Mavis gushed. "We'll invite everyone! Karen's Golden Jubilee! But you must keep your end up!"

Karen was about to suggest what Mavis could do with her end, when her embryonic idea gave a little *kick*. Just a nudge, but she suddenly found herself saying, "Yes, a party. I was thinking the same thing." A smile crept across her lips at Mavis' confused expression. "I still have to work out the details, but I'll get back to you. Have a lovely day, Mavis." Then Karen turned and strode out the door, her thoughts returning to the records in the basement.

"Oh," Mavis stuttered behind her. "Yes, that would be wonderful!"

The confused, frustrated tone of her voice was delicious.

Chapter 3

Karen stood in front of the electric eye, frustrated. She took a step back and approached the door of the grocery door for a third time, but it remained firmly shut. She waved her hand across the sensor: still no result. The wretched things never registered her presence. It had always irritated her, making her think that, perhaps, she didn't really exist.

Resignedly, she brought her purse up and waved it at the sensor. The glass doors parted quietly to let her purse into the supermarket.

Perhaps it only let money in, Karen reflected as she passed into the store. She grabbed a cart and patrolled the aisles, thinking of not existing.

Would it be so bad, really? Not to exist? Not to feel the aches of growing old? Not to feel the despair of losing someone? No betrayal, no failure, no confusion? Just nothingness. A dreamless sleep.

She wandered through the pickle selection, toying with the idea. She quite enjoyed sleeping. She was very good at it. Accomplished, in fact. Very relaxing. When she was young, in one of those dark three a.m. moments when she had considered suicide—funny how now that she was older, she rarely thought about doing it—she had always envisioned overdosing on pills and lying on the bed. No blood, no mess, just sleep. Eternal sleep.

The squeaking wheels of the shopping cart creaked into her thoughts as her mood sank deeper. A sleep so peaceful, so deep, not even that infernal Japanese alarm clock could disturb it.

She pulled up in front of the teas and placed a box of Earl Grey into the cart. She stared at it for a bit before moving on to the cereal section. Eternal sleep would mean no more Earl Grey. No more books, no more Katherine Stone, no more leaves in autumn, no more feeding Mavis misinformation, no chocolate bars, no Tommy, no Jim, no one to feed Mr. Hobbes . . .

Karen shook her head and grabbed a box of cereal.

No way around it, even when you're losing, Life still wins. Too much to be done, whether you want to do it or not. One day, probably when she wasn't looking, it would just end. She stared blankly at the cereal box. End. Her life would simply stop. Like the last page in a book. And on the final page . . . what would be written? *'Karen stepped out onto the street, thinking nothing but how on earth she was going to bake a potato in time for supper when splat! A bus hit her. The End.'*

She gave herself a determined shake and let out a long, heavy breath. Utter nonsense, of course; there were no buses in Little Ivory.

I shall simply have to leave a clause in my will to hire a biographer to ensure my last words are something much more dramatic, she thought, like, *'I've hidden the Rutian Ruby in a box under a tree just by the—ack.'*

Or some fitting Shakespearean quote, perhaps.

Pity she didn't know any.

Karen made a mental note as she hefted a melon: must read some Shakespeare.

She leaned against the cart as her feet sent a tingle of weariness to her brain. Much too early in the day to be entertaining such morbid thoughts. She toddled the cart toward the cafe section, ordered a roast beef—anything but *turkey*, please—sandwich and settled in the nearest seat, determinedly thinking of nothing in particular.

It turned out to be harder than she imagined, thinking of nothing. It was difficult to keep the mind utterly blank in a supermarket. All the people bustling about, the constant voices over intercoms, the clattering of carts; all that racket would prompt a Zen Buddhist to hurl prayer wheels at people.

She saw a young couple strolling along the aisles, their hands clasped as they discussed the pros and cons of what looked like a choice between strawberry or raspberry lemonade. The young brunette woman was revoltingly thin, wearing some pink tank-top type-thing. The man could have walked straight out of one of her books: long hair in a ponytail, wide shoulders, and a nice butt.

Yes, Tommy, mother can still *look*, you know.

Her sons had always treated her as if she was dead from the waist down. Treating her only as "Mom," not as an actual person.

The couple walked into the shelves, and Karen reluctantly removed her gaze from his posterior and gazed around the cafe. Above the head of a bored cashier, infotainment was being shunted across the screen of a silent television.

As a rule, Karen never watched television, barring one or two beloved shows. Such a waste of time, she maintained. She pulled out her reading glasses and carefully positioned them on her nose, where they rested within well-entrenched cavities. As she did so, her eyes flickered to a figure sitting across the cafe from her. Amidst a half-glimpsed head of soft gray hair and plaid fabric, her gaze found a pair of bespectacled soft green eyes.

Locked.

Time melted.

Karen snapped back with a mental start. She fumbled in her purse for a romance novel and schnuffled her nose deep within the pages. Only once she registered that she was holding the book upside-down did she realize that her breathing was irregular and labored, her hands clammy and tight.

Obviously, some sort of attack. Have to see Dr. Johnson about getting some more of those pills he keeps refusing to give me. Probably some form of epilepsy or bizarre foreign ailment I picked up from one of those exchange students in the library or something, because it cannot possibly be the other option . . .

Karen surreptitiously pulled the knife from the table and tilted it in the fluorescent lighting of the cafe to see her face. In its sliver of a reflection, her worst suspicions were confirmed: she was blushing.

Oh, hell.

She slowly replaced the knife and focused her mind determinedly on her book and the story within.

~ φ ~

"Oh Antodus, they'll kill you if they catch you!" Ariadnae gasped as she clutched her lover. The moon above was silver and bright in the night sky. The wind gently caressed the leaves of the olive groves in which they stood. She felt cold and afraid within her cotton robes.

Antodus remained silent as he held her, gently stroking her hair, the filaments of gold slipping between his bare fingers.

Ariadnae took his hand in hers and caressed the scars that the slaver's manacles had emblazoned on his wrist. "Escaped slaves are executed."

"I will die," said Antodus gently. "But first Marcus must pay for his treachery." He kissed her lightly on her forehead. "I have sworn it."

Ariadnae clutched the plaid robes of his toga in her fists. "Why? Why must you insist on killing? We're together again, when we thought we never would be! Isn't that enough?" She felt her eyes fill with tears and cursed herself for her weakness. She pulled her gaze from his deep green eyes and wrenched herself from his grasp, striding along the olive groves—

~ φ ~

Plaid robes? Karen rubbed the bridge of her nose worriedly before continuing.

~ φ ~

Nature seemed to mirror Ariadnae's wrath, as the evening winds gusted through the groves about them. She felt his strong hand on her shoulder, swinging her around to face him once more.

"Wait for me in the courtyard of your villa." His deep green eyes plowed into her soul.

"For your corpse to be delivered to my door?" she asked scornfully.

"By Zeus, I swear I shall be there come morn," he replied, his gaze solemn beneath his mass of silver hair.

"Why should I believe you?" Ariadnae answered hotly. "You've lied to me before."

"Remember our last night together," he responded, his ire rising as the moonlight glinted off his gold-rimmed spectacles. "If that meant anything to you, then you will meet me at dawn." He stepped toward the depths of the grove. "If not, I bid you farewell."

He vanished into the shifting shadows of the trees, leaving Ariadnae to—

~ φ ~

Karen tossed the paperback onto the table with a sigh of frustration.

Glasses in 100 BC indeed!

She cast another glance at the figure at the opposing table as she shoved the novel into her bag.

These books have so many historical inaccuracies in them. Carol Cornell wouldn't make such elementary mistakes. It's hard enough to read them when you've got someone staring at you . . .

Spectacles . . . Plaid togas . . . Ah.

Right.

She pulled a frown at the plastic tabletop in front of her.

Could Day One get much worse?

Probably.

What the hell?

Without giving herself time to think, she gathered up her belongings and walked toward the man's table. As she got closer, waiting for her courage to give way to a nice and predictable bout of good old-fashioned cowardice, she noted his wild silver hair, green eyes and that he was indeed wearing a plaid flannel. And more importantly, she noticed his quite ringless-ring finger. The rest of her mind gave her subconscious a little cheer.

I am going to sit down right there, she told herself as she walked the last of those endless ten feet. Right there. Right in that plastic swivel chair that I'm walking straight past cause I'm a gutless coward and a lonely old woman who has cried herself to sleep so often that there is a crust of salt on my pillow and it's going to be one of those nights again goddamnitohgod . . .

The webbing of her grocery bag snagged the edge of the chair, yanked her off her feet, and deposited a disheveled lump of lonely old lady in the plastic seat, much to the surprise of the man now sitting directly across from her.

Two tables away.

The man looked up from his meal and raised an eyebrow at her sudden, yet distant, arrival.

Karen looked into his eyes and felt the same stomach-swirling emptiness that one feels when falling over a cliff in a dream. Like being swallowed from the inside out, she felt small, helpless, and absurdly stupid.

At that moment, the waitress set a sandwich in front of her.

Karen ripped her consciousness out of the ether or wherever it had got to and stared at the plate before her. Then back at the man.

She hazarded an experimental smile.

The man returned a little grin and lowered his eyebrow.

Just a notch, though.

He smiled back: good teeth. He returned to his meal as Karen continued her appraisal. He didn't appear to be muscular but toned rather than scrawny. His skin was wrinkled like leather, possibly from many years spent working outside. Crinkled eyes twinkled at her like some old thirties' movie Santa Claus.

Karen hefted her own sandwich in both hands but paused, reconsidering the onions and lettuce within. Her front teeth couldn't close completely which always made masticating luncheon meat a bit of a challenge. Particularly when one was being watched.

She took a calculated nibble off a corner wedge.

Pondering how to transition from sly munching and overt staring to actual verbal communication, she was startled to hear someone calling her name.

"Karen?"

The man in front of her hadn't spoken. He was looking over her shoulder.

Karen carefully lowered her sandwich and saw a man standing beside her table.

It can't be.

That voice. That husky timbre . . .

"Eric??"

Familiar wide hands with long delicate fingers held a basket stuffed with wine and cheese. The tiny mole on the side of his nose was the same. The gray eyes still shone as they had in graduate school. Karen had gone back to get her Library Sciences degree after the loss of Michael. She had run into Eric picking out textbooks at the campus bookstore. They had both started graduate degrees late in life and, as strangers in a strange land, had been drawn to each other. The last time she had seen the bearded figure before her, however, was seven years ago after an awkward breakup. And now he was standing in front of her once more.

The only man beside her husband that she had ever loved.

Perhaps Day One wasn't going to be so bad after all.

She looked back to her *object de flirt,* but his chair was vacant, an empty plate and wrinkled napkin the only signs of his fleeting existence.

16

She turned back to Eric Holtz and smiled.

"What on earth are you doing here?" She hoped it didn't sound rude.

"Guest lecturer at our alma mater." He rested his basket on the table. "Turns out getting a degree in Paleontology isn't necessarily a complete waste of time." He frowned at her sandwich. "I'm hoping to get some in-depth research done while I'm here, but I didn't expect to run into you. Do you usually eat in the supermarket?"

"Yes. No. Err . . . I mean, I usually eat with the gals at work, but I'm avoiding work and life in general today." Karen placed the sandwich back on her plate. The stupid thing smelled so good, too.

"What's so special about today?"

"It's my birthday," she paused. "Well, yesterday was, but today is recovery day. And don't even think of asking how old." She glowered.

He raised his hands in a gesture of surrender. "Wouldn't dare."

Damn, that had come out more harshly than she intended. She had forgotten that his degree was in paleontology; she had been too distracted at the time by his other various attributes. Memories of the paleontology department swam before her mind's eye: dusty rooms filled with textbooks and the bones of dead creatures. Still, can't have everything . . .

"I'm going to the Gulf of California this summer to research pigmy woolly mammoths," he continued. "I go there every year."

Before he had even finished his sentence, Karen felt a warm, wide smile spill across her face. The thought, *'I suppose this means I really ought to go to church this Sunday,'* occurred to her, but she shunted it to the back of her mind and settled on mentally sending God a big, fuzzy hug. She took a huge bite out of her sandwich.

"Made it on the cover of *Science* this time round. Hence the lecture this week in Little Ivory," Eric continued. "I've applied for a teaching position here too. I had hoped to run into some of my old college friends, but I had no idea you were still here. What have you been up to?"

Karen found it terribly easy to sum up what she had been doing for the past seven years in a single sentence. So instead, she said, "The boys are fine; Tommy is in the Peace Corps and Jimmy is in the city. Aside from that . . . Her stomach tightened as she recalled how they had split up; he had gotten a postdoctoral position at another university in another state, and while Karen hadn't yet found a job, she had wanted to stay in Little Ivory for the sake of her sons. She hadn't wanted to pursue a long-distance relationship and she had been the one to end it. "The town hasn't changed very much since you left."

Eric grinned a child's cookie-eating grin. "I know. It's fantastic. Grad school was some of the best years of my life. I've been wanting to see everything again."

Her mind experienced a severe contraction and the words, "What are you doing Friday?" flew out of her mouth.

Along with bits of roast beef.

"It would be great to catch up." Eric glanced at his watch and made to rise, perhaps a little nervously? "I'm afraid I must be going. Sorry to rush, I was hoping to meet my assistant, but they haven't shown up and I'm supposed to meet with the Dean this afternoon."

"See you Friday? At Willow Island? Round six?"

"Sounds great. See you then." Eric disappeared through the aisles.

~ φ ~

After some hurried shopping, Karen pulled into her driveway, unlocked the front door, and jumped over a recumbent Mr. Hobbes. She dashed for the phone, spilling groceries over the kitchen counter. As she frantically dialed her best friend's number, she stared blankly at the six frozen pizzas that she had absolutely no recollection of purchasing.

Four rings later, Claire's answering machine picked up. Karen could barely wait for the beep before blurting out, "Claire, are you there? Pick up! It's Eric. Eric Holtz! From college! I've just seen him at the market! Can you believe it? He's gone and found a mammoth. A mammoth! In California! And he's speaking here in town! I haven't seen him in over seven years! I know you've never met him, but I've been going on and on about him for ages. I'm going to go see him on Friday! And he still has the most wonderful eyes and I have six frozen pizzas and I hate those things, so I don't know why I bought them, but isn't it strange? Eric, I mean. Why am I babbling? I hope this tape doesn't run out. It always does when I'm trying to tell you something important!"

A sharp rapping sounded at her front door.

Karen headed down the hallway, the portable still plastered to her ear.

"Oh, hang on a sec, Claire, there's someone at the door, hang on, it will only take a sec. It can't be Mavis, I've already told her off once today, three times if she actually listened to me, it's probably some salesman or something." She was forced to catch the phone in her right hand as it slipped out from the crook of her neck as she flicked back the lock and pulled open the door.

Her dead husband stood on her doorstep.

With flowers.

Claire's tape ended with a quiet *click*.

Chapter 4

Karen's world was warm, fluffy, and safe.

When she opened her eyes the only thing she could see was a gentle tunnel of darkness that ended in a dull yellow orb of light. She had been tucked in this soft haven for an hour now, trying to fall asleep. But now two trouser clad knees blocked her access to the outside world of light and fresh air.

The knees in question belonged to Claire, her best friend. Although nearly a decade younger than Karen, they shared a similar sense of humor and taste for cheesecake. They had become fast friends after being introduced at a knitting group at the county fair several years ago.

"Karen?" Karen felt Claire park herself on a corner of the bed. "Are you okay?"

Karen groaned again, much softer this time.

"I brought ice cream," Claire said. "It's chocolate."

Karen shot out a hand from beneath the covers and snatched the cup from Claire's outstretched hand, then retreated into the dark vestibule.

A long moment of wet slurping passed before Karen heard Claire say, "I have a spoon." The trembling utensil appeared in Karen's field of view.

Karen threw off the covers with a tired sigh. She saw herself in the mirror mounted above the dresser: static-electric-hairdo, streaked mascara, and puffy eyes, all wrapped around a dripping chocolate ice cream goatee.

"Christ!" breathed Claire. "What happened?"

"Life," muttered Karen, wiping her face with a pillowcase. "As usual." She picked up the spoon and started shoveling away. After a few mouthfuls, she saw the room as Claire must see it. It was a mess: pantyhose, books, tissues, and chocolate wrappers lay scattered in Rorschach patterns on the floor, and in some cases, the walls. The blinds were scrunched up and barely covered the windows, letting in orange-red snatches of sunlight.

Karen waved a spoon at the tub of ice cream. "Thanks for this."

"It sounded like an emergency. I know you can't function without dairy during an emergency. It's lucky for you the kids hadn't eaten it yet. So, are you going to tell me or not?"

Karen was silent, her gaze focused on the pint of ice cream.

"I got your message," Claire went on, "but it ended with you opening the door and screaming. I had half a mind to call the police."

Karen did her best Oliver North impression.

"Now look, I've come to help you." Claire said. "I've brought chocolate, as requested, and you've been my best friend for a long time. But if you don't tell me what is going on, I swear by God I'll ram that spoon down your throat!"

Karen gently placed the spoon inside the half-empty container. "Fine, but it is so embarrassing—"

"Spoon . . ." said Claire in a menacingly low voice.

"I opened the front door and standing there was Michael—"

Claire boggled. "Michael? *Michael*, Michael?"

"Yes, Michael, who—"

"Dead Michael? Your **husband**?"

"Yes! Look, spoons can go both ways you know and up both ends, so are you going to let me finish or not?"

"But you told me he was dead!" protested Claire, her neat brown hairdo quivering.

Karen shifted uncomfortably on the bed and pulled the coverlet a little tighter. "Well, sort of."

"Sort of dead?"

"If you really want to know, ten years ago the bastard ran away with my sister Beth." Karen threw the cardboard pint away from her, watching it arc across the room and splat against one of her Monet reprints.

"Oh, Karen," whispered Claire softly. "Why didn't you ever . . ."

"Yes, exactly," muttered Karen. "Painful and horribly embarrassing."

Silence.

"So," ventured Claire eventually. "What did you do?"

~ φ ~

Karen froze.

He stood there, looking like he always had: tight faded blue jeans wrapped around his thick oak-like legs, navy-blue sport coat straining at the seams in a not-so-successful effort to conceal the fact that every square inch of his torso was swathed in muscle. His tiny blue eyes glinted brightly in stark contrast to the dark fur that sprouted in a full beard on his chin. The bastard didn't even have the decency to go bald at fifty with the rest of mankind. His head was still covered with his close-cropped chestnut hair which she remembered running her fingers through, caressing his—

Karen started with a jolt as the realization of what was happening hit her: he wasn't dead or vanished and she truly saw just who was standing on her doorstep, and a decade of hate raged through her and she slapped him full across the face.

She watched with satisfaction as his eyes suddenly snapped wide open as he spun away, the blood spraying upwards as he was knocked back, toppling off the porch and landing in her rose bed.

Blood?

Oh hell. The cordless!

Karen stared at the cracked and blood-soaked phone that was still clenched tightly in her hand, emitting a beeping sound, prompting her to *"Please hang up."* She tossed the phone aside and leapt down the steps to help Michael to his feet.

~ φ ~

"And?" asked Claire, staring at her friend, eyes wide. "Then what? What did he want?"

"I don't know," Karen considered. "He couldn't actually talk, not after—not really . . . I never found out. He just walked away."

"Sounds like the bastard got just what he deserved."

"Well, not exactly." Karen massaged her forehead with her fingertips. "We're going out to dinner tomorrow night at La Grande Poisson."

"What?"

"I had to do something; he was lying there bleeding all over my roses!" She looked up at her friend from between her hands, imploring Claire to understand. "I felt so embarrassed."

Claire picked at a fingernail for a moment. "You're mad, do you know that?"

Karen lay back on the bed, her head flopped over the edge and stared wistfully up at the ceiling. "It has, actually, on occasion, been observed."

"But what about your message?" asked Claire, obviously now thoroughly lost.

"What message?" asked Karen, angling her head upward.

"Your message," Claire said, exasperated. "The guy from grad school. The one you used to go out with?"

"Oh. *That* guy." Karen stared stupidly into space. "You know I have the vague feeling I'm missing something in all this. Something to do with onions . . ."

"Look," said Claire with a sigh, "Mark's out of town, and the kids have probably started eating the chocolate cake for dinner, so I've gotta go." She took Karen's chin in her hand and made her look upside-down into her eyes. "Are you gonna be okay?"

"Me? An aging librarian with a case of arthritis, a not-so-dead husband, and a talent for knocking over valuable objects?" she replied with a tiny smile. "Of course, I'll be fine. Just another chapter in an otherwise thoroughly boring life."

"It never rains," nodded Claire sagely.

"Exactly," said Karen. "Lunch tomorrow?"

"Sure," answered Claire as she rose from the bed. "Noonish?"

"Perfect."

Claire paused at the doorway, looking at the spoon that had somehow become clutched in her hand. "Look," she began awkwardly, "eat some fruit or something, will you?"

Karen flashed Claire a brief smile as she left and propped the pillows behind her against the headboard. She fumbled for the bedside lamp and managed to switch it on, leaving sticky chocolate smears on the brass. She shook her head at the mess and pulled herself out of bed. She grabbed a towel from the cupboard and carefully cleaned her hands before sitting at her desk and reaching for the one thing that always made her feel better.

It had been one of those Sundays. The kind where you're too busy working out what has to be done tomorrow or what to have for dinner to realize what it is. Then, months or perhaps years later you find a photo in a shoebox or stuck in a drawer—a casual snapshot that someone took. And it becomes a symbol of the good old days when times really were better than today.

Karen had found her symbol three years after the divorce. It was wedged on the floor of her wardrobe. She had taken it out again and again over the years until the edges were frayed and white like that of a postcard that had been around the world several times. Emotional mileage. No baggage, please. She pulled out the photograph and stared at it.

The sky was a hazy blue on that summer Sunday, and everyone was squinting in the sunlight. There was Michael, just having mown the lawn, and Tommy and Jimmy holding up their squirt guns with matching grins, as if hunting your sibling was something to be proud of and Karen was on the porch, potato salad in one hand, the other draped on Michael's shoulder.

Karen gazed at her idyllic family and wondered where all the time had gone. She brushed her fingertip over the faces of her two boys before carefully resting the photograph in its box and crawling back under the bed covers.

She grabbed for the nearest romance novel and settled back into her fluffy pillows with a world-weary sigh, laced with hopes that Life would just go away and bother someone else.

~ φ ~

Arthur clashed his blade against Victor's, driving his enemy down the castle steps, hacking and slashing away with every ounce of strength he had left. But Victor parried each blow with the effortless ease of a professional swordsman, a twisted smile stenciled on his face.

Arthur cursed as his blade sparked off the granite blocks of the courtyard wall. He awkwardly brought the blade back to cover to his now open front. The sword swished theatrically through the empty air, but Victor wasn't attacking. He was just toying with the young man.

Victor stood a few paces away, his blade wavering in the candle-lit air, waiting. He waved, mockingly, for Arthur to come closer.

Rage filled Arthur's mind as he leapt once more toward the cretin, and he hacked violently at the man's face, but Victor's steel blade blocked each blow. Again, and again came Arthur, but Victor stood his ground. His face, although filled with interest, showed that he was beginning to grow weary of the proceedings.

With a twirl of his blade, he sent Arthur's sword spinning across the courtyard, to clatter spectacularly on the cobbles. Victor's voice when he spoke, although patient, was serious. "Finished?"

Arthur nodded, his breath labored as he attempted to recover himself, and wiped the sweat from his brow. Victor stepped closer, until their faces were mere inches apart. Victor slipped his palm through the laces of Arthur's shirt and placed his hand on Arthur's breast, just above the heart. Arthur could feel his own racing as Victor brushed his skin.

"Calm yourself, Arthur," said Victor into his ear. "You have much to learn." Their lips touched. Arthur felt his heart thump harder, faster as Victor slipped his other hand down into—

~ φ ~

Karen gave a gasp of shock and hurled the book into her closet at the far end of the room. It landed with a muffled thump in her laundry pile.

Just what, exactly, Karen asked herself in bewilderment, was the library thinking when they accepted those donations from the college bookstore?

Still shaking her head, she switched off the light and rolled over to go to sleep. It was only seven o'clock, but she was forcing the day to end, whether it liked it or not. She closed her eyes and tried to put thoughts of men, all men, including men in tights, out of her head.

Half an hour later, she found herself rummaging in the closet.

Chapter 5

After a cup of the library's terrible coffee, Karen read the obituaries. It wasn't a daily task, as the *Little Ivory Chronicle* was only printed once a month, but it was still the most depressing part of her job as a librarian.

Five years ago, the library board had proudly announced that they now had, countywide, nine thousand card-carrying members. Mr. Brady, the Village Treasurer, pointed out that there were only four thousand people in Little Ivory. Even if every student in the nearby college suddenly became literate, it would only bring the total to eight thousand. A disgruntled Mavis was horrified to discover that over the many years the library had been in business, they had issued library cards for their new members, but had never accounted for their demise.

For each name that Karen crossed out on the *Chronicle* with her black marker, she withdrew a corresponding index card from a drawer. When she reached the bottom of the newspaper, she folded it up and stared at the tiny cards arranged in front of her. One was of a girl who was killed in a hit and run this weekend; she was only fourteen. Her library card record was white and crisp, while the others were old and yellowed. Only fourteen.

The events of yesterday had seemed surreal, unbelievable. This morning, however, Karen was back at work, scowling at Mavis' back. Her life had returned to the familiar routine.

However, the names on the slips of paper in front of her were gone, dead. Kept alive for a few weeks by an antiquated file system.

Karen had felt so exhausted these past few years, she doubted if she would even notice if one of the names she read in the obituaries, one of the cards she pulled, was her own.

No one else would notice. Would they?

Yet yesterday, just for a little while, she had felt alive.

Karen gathered the cards up and carefully put them in a drawer. She had made a decision.

It was time to start doing things on her terms.

Karen looked around the library basement, her hands on her hips, her mind thirty years in the past. The room had an unusually high ceiling, spanned by wooden beams and supported by regularly spaced steel columns. The concrete floor was chipped, and the plasterboard walls were cracked with white chalk dripping from their wounds.

All of that could be hidden with some carefully positioned lighting, Karen decided.

Her main problem, however, were the books. Patrick was already huffing away as he struggled with the first of the boxes of *National Geographic*, although his tone of breath suggested that this activity could not continue for long. Her suspicions were confirmed when he dropped the box to the floor with an agonized moan, sending sprites of dust swirling in every direction.

"All right, Patrick, that's enough, I am well aware of Earth's gravitational pull. You're right, of course, we can't move all of them." Karen gave the nearest box a hearty kick. "Lord knows it's been tried. We've nowhere to put them anyway. We'll have to think of something else."

Patrick gave a grateful little wheeze and slumped, cross-legged to the floor. He propped his head upon his arms and looked about the cellar mournfully.

He'll make a great thespian someday, Karen decided. Only sixteen and miles over the top already. She gave a slight shake of her head and turned back to stare at the rows of tables laden with pulp fiction.

Everyone could donate to the library, even the church. Unfortunately, that left no one for the library to donate *to*. Not even the Head Weeder, Elsa, or anyone else on the library staff, including Karen, could simply throw out, burn, or destroy a book. Some sort of Bibliocratic Oath or something. Karen was rather proud of their unspoken and united philosophical stand on this issue in some way, but the end result of such a policy was a library filled to the metaphorical teeth with utterly useless books.

The door at the far end of the room creaked open to reveal the figure of Claire backlit by a rare flash of morning sun. Claire carefully pushed the steel door shut and joined them to stare at the pile in the middle of the floor.

"We're trying to decide what to do with several thousand magazines, pulps, and outdated nonfiction texts. Short of a bonfire, that is." Karen pulled herself to her feet and glanced at her watch. "You're just in time."

Claire rested her handbag on the floor. "I thought perhaps Mulligan's today?"

"In time to help, I mean," said Karen, a sense of purpose filling her voice. "Patrick, go and get a few rolls of tape, would you? We've got work to do."

Patrick nodded and leapt up off his improvised stool. He dashed up the stairs to the main lobby.

"I've just left work," said Claire pointedly. "This is supposed to be my lunch 'break,' remember?"

"Don't worry," said Karen, waving her hands as she marched around the boxes. "I've ordered our lunch from that Greek place you like so much." She stopped at a randomly selected box and hefted it up in her arms.

"Really? When was that?"

"In about ten minutes or so I should think. I should find the phone number by then." Karen headed toward the wall. "Come on, grab a box."

Claire let out a sigh and heaved at a box of Sidney Sheldon's. "She bribed me with gyros, so I must do her bidding."

"That's the spirit!" Karen stacked another box filled with *Geographics*, images of colorful birds and natives staring out from within their yellow borders. With a heave, she spilled the contents out onto the cement floor, scattering slim magazines and digests that bounced and slid against the table legs.

Patrick hopped down the stairs, his arms full of tape rolls.

"Thank you, Patrick," said Karen, grabbing the tape out of his arms. "Now," she indicated to the nearest tower of boxes, "line all those boxes along the walls. We're going to make a new wall. It shortens the room a bit, but at least we can get some of them out of the way."

Karen noticed Patrick's significant look at the workload arrayed around him, but she studiously ignored him and continued chatting to Claire. He started stacking the books in silence, broken only by the occasional grunt.

Karen tossed a roll of tape into Claire's arms. "Tear off all the good covers and post them up on the boxes. Mind you, none of those ones with the bare-chested native women, or Elsa will have some sort of fit." She paused, a collection of magazines in her arms. "On second thought, that might be rather fun . . ."

"And what will you be doing?" Claire asked.

"The north wall should probably be *Life*, I think. Hmm? Oh, ordering lunch, of course. I don't know about you, but I'm starving!" Karen headed for the stairs, carefully stepping over the magazines.

Claire stared at the rainforest of animals, cars, faces, and landscapes arrayed at her feet. "I thought you didn't want to destroy them?"

Karen paused on the stairwell, a hand on the steel banister. "Don't worry, we've got those in triplicate down here. Probably more actually." She started up the stairs again before pausing once more. "Try and find any with 1940s pictures on them. It's not very likely, but it would be nice. Better luck with *Life* probably," she continued to herself. "Sheep or chicken?"

"I beg your pardon?" asked Claire.

"Gyros," explained Karen.

"Oh, sheep, please," responded Claire.

"Did you ever know that you're my gyro?"

Claire sat down in a metal folding chair and resignedly started ripping the covers off the magazines. "I hope the food is better than your puns."

~ φ ~

Karen looked up from affixing the last of the magazine covers to the wall as she heard the door to the main library swing open. A stumpy woman wrapped mostly in tweed with auburn hair descended the staircase, her eyes darting from one corner of the basement to the other.

"What do you think?" Karen stepped back from the wall, wiping the dust off her hands and onto the sides of her slacks.

The floor was still gray and bare as it had been a few hours before, but now the walls were a billboard of images of times and places and people that represented cultures and ages long past. Buster Crabbe stared out from beneath a portrait of an unknown girl by an abandoned farm in the Dust Bowl, while a sixty-seven

Chevy sat gleaming in all its chrome glory on a stretch of highway. Hundreds of faces and places looked out onto the concrete floor.

"You've been busy." Elsa crossed over to a picture of Gene Autry.

Karen took the moment to shift herself so that she stood in front of the photograph of topless Ethiopian villagers. "Yes, well, Patrick got a bit carried away after the first few hours. I expect he's passed out upstairs somewhere. Still, got most of it done. Just that bit left over there," she said, waving to a corner that remained bare of pictures.

"What goes there?" Elsa wandered over to the corner.

"A band, if I can talk Oscar's lot into it, but probably just a turntable." Karen knelt to collect the empty rolls of tape and scissors.

"A dance? I thought so, but I wasn't sure. Why didn't you just say so? We had one last Christmas."

Karen paused, stuffing the rubbish into empty paper bags. "Ahh . . . that was just a dance. This will be a Dance!"

Elsa wiggled her nose.

"Real dancing," Karen continued. "None of this jiggling and nonsense they do today, but *dancing*. Nothing but the Andrews Sisters, Glen Miller . . ."

"Oh, please," protested Elsa. "You weren't even alive when he was playing."

"No one under fifty allowed," Karen replied firmly.

"Will you make an exception so that I can come?" teased Elsa.

"Ha, ha." Karen tied up the last bag of trash.

"So that's what this is about," said Elsa, eyeing her. "You're feeling old. You want something to do so that you don't have to think about it. I believe this is termed 'distraction behavior.'"

"I hardly think holding a party to celebrate my age is avoiding the issue," Karen countered. "Besides, no one's using this room Friday, are they? The decor is free and probably the music. Have to do something about the lighting in this place, though . . . It's just that there's so little in this town for us . . . *mature* people to do on a Friday night, isn't there?"

Elsa raised both hands in the air in mock surrender. "It's fine by me, Karen. I think it sounds like an excellent idea. It's Mavis you should worry about. You know, letting people have fun and all that in her library. She's never been very keen on the public."

"Oh, don't worry," said Karen. "It was her idea, or at least she'll think it was by the time she hears about it. What time is it anyway? I'm exhausted."

"I'm not sure. Almost six, I think."

"Six!" Karen jumped to her feet, then winced as her back screamed in protest.

"Yes, I think so. What's the matter?"

"I've got a—" Karen almost said the word "date." In fact, she had wanted to scream it to the world for about twenty-four hours now, even if it was only with Michael. But going into particulars would be difficult, even to Elsa. "—an appointment . . . with Claire . . . to see that new movie."

"Sounds like fun . . . pity some of us have to work. I've got the evening shift tonight at the reference desk. Have fun." Elsa stooped to examine some of the photos.

"I'm sure it will be . . . interesting." In truth, Karen still had no idea why Michael was back. She wasn't entirely certain she wanted to know. She strode up the stairs and out into the main lobby. She paused by the main desk, puzzled. Surely, she had forgotten something.

From downstairs came a startled shriek.

Ah, she thought. Amazonian tribesmen bathing. *National Geographic*, 1934.

Patrick jumped up in alarm from his seat at the checkout counter. "What was that?"

"Oh, I'm probably just going to Hell, that's all," said Karen, a little smirk on her lips as she walked out of the library.

Chapter 6

Karen sat before the mirror, a pink plastic brush clutched tightly in her hand as she peered at her reflection that no longer seemed familiar. Too many lines to begin with, and too much of the rest of her for another. Another person staring back.

Fifty.

Not old enough to have seen the Andrews Sisters.

Not old enough to have danced to a real forties swing band.

But old enough to realize how to treat people. To realize how nasty she had been to Elsa. To know what it was like to be hurt.

Old enough to know better.

Karen carefully placed the brush down on the counter, her eyes avoiding her own gaze. She would take down any offending photographs in the library tomorrow, nude, lewd, or otherwise. She glanced at the opposite wall of her bedroom still plastered with the streaked remains of chocolate lumps that marred the *"Wedding Dress Cream"* of her duvet.

Still there.

All the events of yesterday actually happened: fit of depression, mystery man, mammoth-hunter, dead husband, and all. Great.

And the not-dead husband would be here at eight then.

To take her on a date.

Karen began to wonder at exactly what point she had gone insane.

She picked up her hairbrush once more. She gently passed the brush through her hair, gray and sandy strands that had once glowed a luxurious brown.

And the Himalayas had once been a series of low hills.

She felt something warm and furry rub against her leg and looked down to see Mr. Hobbes glaring back at her.

"Sorry, hon." She scooped the malleable mass of fur up in her arms. "I'll get your dinner out soon, but you're on your own tonight." She dumped him on the counter as she walked to the bath. He started lapping happily at the faucet in the sink, his tail flicking in the air.

~ φ ~

Her fingers fumbled blindly with the buttons on his shirt as they kissed, their mouths full of tongues, skin, and laughter. His wedding ring glinted in the light of the lamps as he carried her across the room. His thin steel-gray tie caught in her teeth, as she playfully bit through the open fabric and gnawed at his chest hairs. She let out a little squeal as they fell upon the bed. Her left shoe slipped off, clattering across the hardwood floor.

Their eyes were one now, their faces inches apart, but neither blinked. They remained still, not breathing, each realizing what was about to happen, each daring the other to make the final move.

A wicked grin crept across his face. Her arms were inside his shirt now, his breath on her face, and she found herself laughing too. She felt his hand slide along her thigh, pulling her to him . . .

~ φ ~

The mighty hunter crept along the ledge, sniffing the new scents wafting through the air. He licked his lips, removing the last drops of water as he approached the thing, his tail high in the air, twitching with excitement. His head held low, he slowly padded closer.

The thing was small, round, and filled with new smells. He flared his nostrils as he crept nearer, inhaling the interesting scents. It rested near the edge of the cliff and was about level with his nose now, but sat unmoving, obviously unaware of its predator.

He nudged it cautiously with a paw and started as it glided away. It came to rest a few inches away, its edges trembling. Ears back, he raised his haunches. His tail twitched furiously, poised for action. Then he flew through the air with a triumphant leap, claws extended, and pounced on the thing.

It exploded at his touch. The flurry of white powder caused him to fall backward in surprise. He knocked the pad into the toilet and tumbled into the bathtub.

The water erupted in a spray of bubbles, arms, legs, claws, and loofahs as he and Servant-Woman let out a series of screams and thumps. Shampoo and conditioner bottles rained down upon them as Servant-Woman fumbled for a handhold and he fought desperately for a claw-hold.

He was the first out of the tub, followed by a series of yells and curses as Servant-Woman clutched her bleeding limb with her other hand. He bolted through the house and hid behind the dryer, shivering with the cold, his fur sticky and spiked from the dreaded water.

~ φ ~

Karen hauled herself out of the bathtub with one hand and grabbed for a towel with the other, pressing it against her clawed arm. She stood there shivering for a moment as water pooled about her feet. Her fuzzy make-up pad floated in the toilet. Still dazed, she reached into the tub and pulled out the remains of the novel she had been reading. She was tempted to ring out the water like a rag but dropped it on the countertop instead.

Typical. Just when it was getting interesting.

The next ten minutes were a blur of slacks, dresses, and bandages as she ripped her closet apart to find something to wear for the dat—dinner. She finally settled on a simple pair of slacks and a blouse that managed to cover the clawed areas while still revealing enough to remind Michael of what he had been missing for the past ten years.

She stood before the mirror, her face flushed from her frantic efforts, and stared in dismay at her hair—hair which she had painstakingly kept clear of the tub water—which was now doing its best clown impression.

"Hobbes, you are *soooo* dead!"

Mr. Hobbes, upon hearing his name mentioned in a manner that suggested neither tuna treats nor warm snuggles, bolted from the laundry room and ran like hell for the cat flap in the front door.

Briefly entertaining the idea of switching kitty litter for quicksand, Karen rummaged through her drawers for hairpins. As her hands fumbled with the mess before the mirror, she pondered, What do I care what I look like anyway? After all, he's my *ex*-husband; the papers were signed, they had moved on. He hadn't shown his hide in years. It wasn't as if they were going to *do* anything? Right?

Certain portions of her lower body sent their votes on what they thought on the subject. She stared at her reflection, suddenly not sure of anything anymore.

Which was, of course, when the doorbell rang.

Mr. Hobbes sat upon the windowsill by the front door and stared at his nemesis with obvious disdain.

Michael stared at the cat, an expression of loathing on his face. He shifted his feet impatiently and pressed the doorbell again. He gingerly fingered his nose as he glared at the cat, daring Mr. Hobbes to look away first.

Mr. Hobbes swished his tail distractedly but didn't blink.

"Cats only stare at each other as a threat." Karen had been able to see the exchange through the window. "He thinks you're going to attack."

The look on Michael's face seemed to say, *'Chance would be a fine thing.'* He turned to Karen, a worried frown on his face, but it cleared when she held up her hands to show she was unarmed.

"Hi, Karen."

"Hello, Michael." Karen pulled the door shut behind her with a thud. She stood before him, her hands clasping her purse.

There was an awkward silence.

"This is where you say how nice I look," prompted Karen.

Even if I do look like something found in Mr. Hobbes' litter box.

"Sorry. You look fantastic, of course." Michael moved toward the car, and then paused, facing her once more. "You're taking this much better than last time."

Karen raised an eyebrow. "You've lost the element of surprise, that's all." She walked to his Camaro and slid into the passenger seat. "Don't worry, I still loathe you with every fiber of my being."

"I'm just glad you're unarmed." Michael moved behind the wheel.

Karen stroked her purse that contained a three-quarter-inch adjustable wrench but decided not to mention it.

Michael reversed the car out of the driveway and headed down the main road. Karen gave Mr. Hobbes a little wave as they sped away, but the cat merely hopped off the windowsill in disgust and started skulking about in the front bushes.

Karen shrugged.

Nothing a little bacon couldn't cure. If only the rest of her problems could be so easily solved.

They drove on in silence. Maples and oaks stretched a fluttering green ceiling across the road, letting the heavy blues of twilight slip across the windshield. The only sound was the slight hum of the engine as the car flew along the country lanes and back roads. As the sun set, fields full of dozing cows flashed by as the sky grew darker and blacker until the silhouettes of cows turned into bizarre black lumps and outcrops. Karen found herself watching the yellow center stripes pop out of the darkness ahead, fighting to think calm and reasonable thoughts. Trying not to ask the questions she wanted to ask. Questions he never answered.

They weren't really complex questions either, nothing more than the Why, What, When, How, and Where variety. She knew the Who bit and, to be honest, she didn't really want to know the answer to the How Often. Simple questions, really, but she wasn't sure she was quite prepared for the answers. Even today.

The more obvious question of '*What-the-hell-am-I-doing-here?*' flashed into her head for the hundredth time.

Still silence.

Karen remembered this silence. She had endured it during the last five years of their marriage. The vacuum in which each person had a million questions, but neither dared ask. It always made her throat dry and made her stomach twist and retch. She had forgotten how physically sick it made her feel. A silence that could be cut with a knife.

Or perhaps with a rusty wrench?

"Don't you want to know why I'm back?" he asked.

Karen snapped her head round from the window in surprise and stared at his profile, her thoughts racing. Of course, I want to know why you're back. I'm dying to know why you've showed up again you lousy—

"To be honest, I don't think I do," she responded eventually. She turned back to the window, searching for more bovine ink-splotches.

"Really?" he asked.

"Do I want to know why you're here? I assume that you either want something or have something particularly unpleasant to tell me, or both, otherwise you would have simply phoned—"

"You always used to hang up on me—" Michael protested.

"Or left a message on my machine," she continued, unperturbed. "So, do I want to hear something unpleasant? No, quite honestly, I don't. I will, however, tell you why *I* think you are here. I think that you are here to buy me a very expensive dinner, following which, you will apologize profusely for the numerous past injustices that you have caused me over several slices of chocolate cake. I will then refuse to listen and then insult you in a devastatingly witty way and I shall stalk away leaving you to hate yourself for having ever left me."

Michael roared with laughter at that and swung them round the final curve and into the parking lot of La Grande Poisson. "I'm just glad that you're not bitter."

"Not at all," replied Karen sweetly. "Now, shall we eat?"

~ φ ~

La Grande Poisson was a converted barn that sat atop a hill in what passed for the middle of nowhere in Little Ivory. The wooden slats of the outer walls had been painted rich shades of forest green, while the inside was stained a rich lacquered brown. The adjoining house served as the kitchen, while a jazz quartet, nestled high up in the loft, played soft, sad notes that drifted down to the main dining area. Circular tables were adorned with candles that sprouted from wine bottles.

In keeping with the farmhouse motif, straw was artfully placed along the floors and interwoven with the antique farming implements that hung from the walls. The chairs were wicker, the tablecloths plaid, and the menu contained food from almost every culture that could be priced above sixty dollars. The restaurant attracted rich people from the city who wanted a taste of the simple life, but only the best bits. Mrs. Marple, the owner, was happy to provide whatever they might want, for the right price.

All Karen really wanted was the roast duck and said so.

"I'll have the New York strip steak," said Michael, handing the unused menus to Matt, Mrs. Marple's eldest, who was their waiter for the evening.

"The house wine?" prompted Matt, as he poured their waters.

"Umm . . ." Michael pondered for a moment until catching Karen's steely gaze. "Probably not, really," he answered to Matt, as he placed a basket of bread on their table. "Bring the best that you have."

Ahh, the awkward silence between bread and salad, Karen thought. After this I shall write a book on *How Not to Kill Your Ex-Husband, However Tempting It May Be*. Guaranteed bestseller.

Her gaze lingered on the fine and pointy silverware until she placed her elbows over the tempting cutlery. She rested her head upon her hands and stared wistfully into the candle; it was one of those purple-black ones scented with some flowery stuff. The flame twittered about its long wick, isolated in a deep pool of molten wax.

Karen felt a great deal of empathy for that little flame.

She blinked herself out of her stupor and stared across the table at her ex-beloved. This was not a divorce trial; they weren't young anymore. She could be civilized and make conversation with another human being. She could handle this.

Karen took a deep breath and plunged in.

They talked the small talk: how were the kids, alimony, irritating relatives, in-laws, and about how little Little Ivory had changed over the years. They discussed how all those little pains had started flaring up, how people at diners had started giving them senior discounts. As the salad came and went and the wine was refilled, the words poured out and splashed back and forth between them, not exactly with loving tenderness, and there was a tendency to hedge around large and obviously restricted grounds of conversation, but friendly just the same.

At one point, as Karen hacked away at a particularly difficult bit of duck, she realized that she had forgotten that they had ever talked this way, that they really were once close friends. She took a thoughtful pull at her wine glass as she mulled that over.

She put the glass down and took a mental step back. Michael was sawing away at his steak and talking animatedly about how the business had been taking an upturn what with the end of that War and all. Forks and bits of food stabbed the air for emphasis.

This is all wrong, she thought, horribly, horribly, wrong.

Karen finished off the last of her duck and waited until ordering coffee before she bolted for the women's room.

Chapter 7

Back again, eh? Karen's reflection seemed to ask.

Shut up you.

The mirror was one of those obscenely wide ones that rested above a series of sinks in the shape of metal basins. The soap dispensers were cow udders matching the stalls behind her that were designed to look like stables. She pulled at her hair and adjusted her blouse distractedly.

Okay. What is the next step? Be nice and polite and let him take us back home and . . . what? She started rubbing her brow with her hands in irritation before she remembered that it was a nervous habit that she had been trying to break for . . .

For ten years.

She stared through her trembling fingers as the memory flooded back, flooding her mind and washing out the sounds of the restaurant and the people and crashing against her. She clung to the wash basin as she staggered against the power of—

~ φ ~

She slowly eased open the front door and slipped inside, careful, as always, not to let the screen door bang shut behind her. She wore a matching dark blue blouse and skirt with bracelets that dangled from her wrists. Her hair was swept up in a Katharine Hepburn style, her lips painted a striking red. The necklace that her sons had given her for her birthday sparked in the light from the chandelier as she crept through the hallway.

Her sharp heels dug into the plush carpet as she strode up the stairs to their bedroom. A deep bass thump of music reverberated through the house. One gloved hand gently gripped the railing while the other held the tickets to the opening night of Porgy and Bess.

She passed the children's rooms, vacant and empty now that summer camp had claimed its latest victims. She tilted her head toward the white paneled door of her bedroom, listening to the trickle of music leaking from within. With a grin on her face, she pushed the door open, tickets high in the air, her voice already vibrating with a "Surprise!"

They lay on her bed. He was astride her, his chest glistening with sweat, his face blood red with exertion, his eyes closed, lips pressed tight. She lay beneath him, jiggling and moaning as he thrust and humped, pushing her against the headboard. She had her hands grasping his buttocks, pulling him into her deeper and deeper, faster and faster.

Her bed . . . Her headboard . . . Her husband . . . Her SISTER! Karen held her trembling hands up to her face and stared at the scene in horror.

They only stopped when they heard her scream.

~ φ ~

Karen felt the cool porcelain press against her cheek as she focused on the present once more. Squinting in distaste at the smell, she flushed the toilet, pulled herself off her knees and pushed the stall door open with a white and sticky hand. She walked back to the sink and rinsed out her mouth. She cleaned up her chin, brushed her hair down and tweaked her cheeks to bring some color back, but she couldn't look her reflection in the eye.

She didn't have a plan. But she had the confidence to think of one, which was half the battle after all.

Pity about the duck though.

She walked out the bathroom door and marched straight to the payphone.

40

Chapter 8

When she returned to the table, Karen was afraid that she wouldn't be able to even look at the chocolate cake. She had to eat it; she wasn't going to give Michael the slightest hint of the effect he had on her. Fortunately, after having lost most of her one hundred and twenty-eight-dollar dinner, she was ravenous. She tucked into the cake with gusto.

She was happily chomping away when Michael took a deep drink of his coffee and frowned at the bill.

"Look," he began, "I think this is where I say I'm sorry."

"Yes," replied Karen around a mouthful of Black Forest. "And this is where I ignore everything you're about to say." She flashed him a tight smile, but her tone held dark undercurrents.

"I know that nothing I can say can ever be enough to . . ."

"No," cut in Karen sharply. "It can't." She placed her fork calmly on her empty plate and tossed the napkin on top. She closed her eyes and went on. "There isn't enough time in the universe or pain in the world for you to be sorry enough," she told him, her voice increasing in volume. She opened her eyes and looked at him. "Because you haven't been forced to live alone for the past ten years, to know what that's like or what it's like to have to raise the family while you go around doing whoever and whatever you damn well please!" She caught herself yelling. She lowered her voice and leaned back in her chair. "You can't even try and if you did you would do it badly. Just like everything else you've ever done."

Michael's eyes widened. He opened his mouth to speak, but she cut him off before he had a chance.

"And if you please," Karen went on. "I'd like to go home now."

"At least you've stuck to your schedule." Michael slipped some cash into the billfold and turned around to hand it to Matt as he passed by. "Isn't this the bit where you say some 'devastatingly witty remark'?"

Karen acted quickly, without thinking. With one hand, she dumped the remains of his coffee into her own cup, and made a quick motion with her other hand. She fervently hoped he wouldn't notice the smell.

The flame sputtered, but remained lit.

As Michael turned back around, she smiled sweetly and stood up. "Thanks for dinner," she said, tossing back the remains of her coffee as she did so. Michael stood up as well, tossed back the contents of his mug, and swept up the two dinner mints with his other hand.

Karen looked on curiously as Michael's face went beat red. He started to make an entertaining gurgling sound. The mints went flying as he started clutching at his throat, retching as the molten wax contents solidified on his tongue, teeth, and throat.

"Sorry," called Karen as she left for her cab. She walked around Matt, who was mistakenly attempting to give Michael the Heimlich maneuver. "Change of plan. I couldn't think of a single witty thing to say."

~ φ ~

Wilbur, Little Ivory's only taxi driver, was thrilled to have a fare. However, he wouldn't stop asking questions about her night, until Karen offered him ten dollars to spend the rest of the ride in silence. She approached her front door cautiously, but it was thankfully free of policemen or trench-coated FBI agents. She snuck into her kitchen and tossed a bag of popcorn into the microwave. Then, her fingers sticky from the buttery bag, she crept into the living room, snuggled in an afghan, and watched the ten o'clock news.

A special report of twice-dead husbands was not sandwiched between the news of the latest border conflicts and political scandals.

Relief washed through her as she realized she probably hadn't actually killed Michael after all. She popped in a VHS tape and blankly watched the latest version of Titanic. She caught herself nodding off before the iceberg hit and decided to call it a night.

As Karen climbed into bed, she wondered why the vision of a dead Michael disturbed her so much. After all, it was exactly what she had been telling everyone for years; she even managed to get paid vacation in the form of Grief Days out of Mavis in October.

Yet she had always known that the wretched man was completely and utterly not dead and probably living life in wondrous ways that she had never—and would never—experience.

"I guess," she told Mr. Hobbes as he settled in the crook of her legs on top of the eiderdown, "you should be careful what you wish for." He cocked his head slightly as he was addressed, then resumed grooming himself. "Funny," she continued, "I always told Tommy and Jimmy those clichés. They always thought I was talking nonsense. So did I, really. Who knew I would be right?"

Mr. Hobbes, apparently realizing that sleep was not an immediate option, stood up from his half-curl and walked up the fluffy hills of her body, resting his two front paws on her shoulder to stare at her.

"Sorry about dinner," she apologized. "Things got a little bizarre."

Mr. Hobbes nuzzled her chin.

Karen let out a little squeak of laughter as she brushed his head away and wiped off the cat drool. She scratched his head, stroked his back, and listened as the purring dramatically increased in volume. Amazing the power that bacon has.

Mr. Hobbes nestled against her side as Karen reached up and switched off the reading lamp. Doing so, she noticed she still had smudges of chocolate on her hands.

A dinner of cake and popcorn.

I'm probably going to pay for that.

Chapter 9

Karen was running.

Creaks and groans followed her as she ran. The planks were soaked with sea water that kept causing her to lose her footing. Yet every time she fell, her hand caught the counter tops, and she managed to keep running as the floor became the wall and the wall the ceiling.

With a crack, the world righted itself.

She slammed to the floor on her side, but her body felt no pain.

When she raised her head, she could see that Elsa and the waiter from La Grande Poisson were sitting at a table above her, talking animatedly and sharing a burrito.

The walls of the restaurant had been replaced with glass. Outside, Karen could see turbulent waves of water smashing against the panes. The glass panels fractured, forming cracks that started spider-webbing outward under the tremendous pressure.

Staggering to her feet, she realized that the restaurant had snapped in half. The kitchen had fallen into the ocean and all that she could see behind the counter was the frothy hell of the sea.

But there was someone clinging to the cash register behind the counter. It was a figure—a man—but she couldn't make out whom it was. For some reason, she started to stagger toward him.

The other customers didn't seem to notice that their restaurant was sinking into the Atlantic; they kept eating and sipping soda as they slipped toward death. The penguins seemed pretty upset though. She had to fight her way past flocks of the streaming Antarctic birds as she hauled herself, table by table, to the man, who was scrambling against the sea, his hands clawing desperately at the cash drawer.

He couldn't hold on.

Her feet kept slipping.

Two of the penguins careened into her and dragged her to the floor in their panic.

She wasn't going to make it.

There was a lurch as the restaurant slammed against another willow tree and Karen was flung toward the counter.

She managed to grasp his wrist just before he slipped into the waves.

She braced her feet against the counter wall and *heaved*.

He burst out of the water and sprawled on top of her like a wet fish.

And she could see his face.

It was the boy with floppy red hair.

The boy she had seen in her dreams exactly six times in her fifty-year life. Once, when she was seventeen, she had a quick flash of him loading a bag into the trunk of his car, laughing at some joke and she had known in that instant that this was the literal man of her dreams, whom she had searched for her whole adult life. He had appeared again the night after she had been in the car accident, a soft red blur that went past as he flashed away on a bike. He was the reason why she did a double take whenever she saw a redhead in the library. Her breath still caught in her throat any time she thought a stranger on the street might turn out to be him.

He had been bowling with her on Broadway, blown up planets with her in the far reaches of space, and now he was drowning in a Taco Palace in the Atlantic Ocean.

She had dreamt his laughter, felt his touch and seen his floppy red hair, but she had never, ever seen his face.

He looked down at her now, his hair plastered against his freckled visage, and she could see for the first time that his eyes were a brilliant emerald green.

He still looked like he was seventeen.

And then the wave front hit them, and Karen screamed in shock as he was pulled from her arms and into the darkness of forever and her mouth filled with salt water as time went molten around her.

~ φ ~

Karen woke up on the floor wrapped in her sheets and bathed in sweat.

Her mouth was filled with her tear-soaked pillow.

She realized she was shivering.

Chapter 10

Karen set the glob of dough into a bowl and covered it with a cloth. Carefully removing dashes of flour from the counter with a towel, she washed her hands before settling into the living room to wait for the bread to rise. The library didn't even open until one o'clock on Wednesdays, so she had plenty of time. She was never entirely sure why this was so but suspected that it was Mavis' intent to not be *too* convenient for the public, as they were getting the service they paid for. A tip jar on the checkout counter would surely appear in the near future.

Karen, a fan of sleeping in whenever possible, was hardly one to complain. Wednesdays were traditionally her day to putter around the house and do piddly chores. Although she was never particularly domestic, kneading and baking the odd loaf always made Karen relieve some stress and had the added benefit of giving the house a nice 'lived-in' feel. Not to mention, while the yeast bacteria worked their little magic, it was the perfect time to settle down with a good book.

Or, like today, to savor some more of *Eternal Passions VIII*, still store-shelf fresh.

~ φ ~

Kate slammed the empty mug on the table and stared haughtily at the man across the bar. Her white blouse slipped off her shoulder with the motion, and she felt his eyes on the crimson-purple scar that marred her milk-fresh flesh. Boiled water had splashed across her skin as a baby, leaving a stain that was frozen forever to her shoulders and back. She had hidden the scarring through her youth, but now she wore it as a trophy, enjoying people's stares and discomfort. Its color and implied pain contrasted the beauty of her face, golden hair, ample bosom, and athletic figure.

The bar was gloomy and poorly lit. Flickering lanterns glinted off exposed flesh, coins, and carefully brandished weapons. The youth of the city clustered in this den of iniquity to mingle and gab. The noise was deafening.

The man across from her was dark, swarthy, and muscular; lust dripped from every pore.

Just the way Kate liked them.

But tonight, she sought a prize other than flesh.

Dr. Katherine Stone had done her research; this was the man she wanted. Upon receiving the ransom note, she had left Enrique, her latest lover, and made her way to India. At the University of Delhi, Kate scoured every drawing and map of the Subcontinent that she could get her hands on until her desk was buried from a veritable cartographic blizzard. She had poured over every sheet, attempting to decipher the puzzle. She called in favors with her colleagues in the Geography Department until she had finally managed to procure the map for which she had been searching for so long: the map that showed the route to the Caves of Alexander.

Logan, the man in front of her, was the only one with the Cobra Codex that would allow her to decipher the map and lead her to the lost caves.

The caves where they had taken her father.

~ φ ~

Lost fathers.

Dead husbands.

Karen settled back in her recliner and frowned at a dusty spider web that clung to the lampshade. She felt uneasy. She wasn't sure she had handled the Michael situation correctly. She desperately wanted to know why he had returned but couldn't give him the satisfaction of actually *telling* her. But that wasn't what was truly bothering her. She was prepared to turn fifty, barely, but not to deal with this mess.

Not-dead husbands.

Paleontologists.

Slutty sisters.

How was one meant to deal with this sort of thing?

It all sounded so much like a plot in a bad . . .

Oh.

Fudge.

~ φ ~

Ding.

The little oven bell announced that the bread was done and so was Karen's latest research project. Her dining room table was covered with novelettes emblazoned with covers of embraces, pink skin, flowing hair, dark eyebrows, tanned skin, chiseled chins, and half-closed lids lined with perfect eye shadow. While it looked chaotic, there was a method to her fractal grouping.

Karen did not seriously expect to gain any valuable insight from her sorting; she did it to relax. Sorting and indexing was a Zen art form gained from library-ing that helped her collect her thoughts. Her organization frenzy only applied to books, not to the ghastly mess that was her hall closet. If nothing else, the project helped her weed out which books she was going to donate to the thrift store.

She had amassed the selected works into three rough piles. The first featured innocent housewives living in small towns. After casual perusing, she decided that these provided little useful knowledge. She was terribly familiar with small town life and as far as she was aware, there were no new studs riding down Main Street on their horse, motorcycle or, in one odd instance, a snowmobile.

Pile Two was somewhat more promising: jilted lovers, cross-indexed with sisters and alphabetized by form of betrayal. Karen was rather proud of Pile Two. However, jilted though she may feel, her sister was not, as far as she knew, within a hundred miles, and it didn't help her work out what to do with Michael, mammoth hunters, or tracking down the supermarket flirtation. As small as the town was, no one knew everyone, unfortunately.

On to Pile Three. As far as piles went, it was interesting from a psychological perspective. She was somewhat taken aback by the sheer number of supposedly dead ex-husbands returning from wars/Russia/Darkest Peru to wreak havoc with the new love life of the unsuspecting widower motifs.

Which made Karen just a little uneasy, for perhaps she may have inadvertently drawn inspiration from her books in Michael's demise, then, logically perhaps, she had subconsciously known that complications could arise upon his return.

Perhaps using romance novels as a Survival Guide was not the best of ideas.

Karen buttered a slice of the raisin bread and watched the golden oil seep into the warm spongy brown pores as she savored

48

the smell of cinnamon. This wasn't working. She still felt old and completely at a loss of what to do next.

What would Dr. Katherine Stone do?

Chapter 11

A light babble of voices floated around the pub, vying with clouds of smoke for dominance. The early lunch crowd of the retired and the unemployed sat at little wooden tables, while the bartenders cleaned up the glasses and pitchers from the night before. Hazy sunlight from the frosted glass windows cast impressionistic shadows on the flagstone floor, giving an almost church-like feel to the *Fleur de Coeur*.

"Hello there!"

Karen raised her head and eyed the new arrival carefully. It was Emma, the latest Children's Librarian. Emma was a bright, educated, and confident young woman from England who did what she wanted. She had traveled the world living out of a backpack for a year and was first in her class at college.

She was everything that Karen wasn't.

Karen had liked her from the first minute they met.

She smiled as her friend slid into the chair across from her.

"Happy birthday!" enthused Emma as she set her beer on the table.

Karen's smile faltered.

"What's the matter? It's your birthday, isn't it?" Emma pulled her thick, black hair, apparently still damp, up into a pile on top of her head.

"It was. I'm older today. I'm past fifty now."

"So how old are you?"

"Fifty years and three days."

"Oh," said Emma, slightly puzzled. "How long have you been here then?" She gestured around the pub.

Karen glanced at her watch. "Since ten, I think."

"Why?"

Because Dr. Katherine Edwards always had a pint when she was trying to solve a mystery. Instead, Karen admitted, "I'm trying to feel young."

"In a bar?"

"Isn't this what young people do?" Karen asked. "I never did it, but I have heard it's quite the thing."

"Yeah," Emma said slowly. "But when old people do it . . . it's well . . . scary somehow." She took another sip from her drink. "I mean, kids see old people hanging around bars looking to pull, and you just think to yourself, 'God I hope that's not me in thirty years,' right?"

Emma was blissfully unaware of the effect her words were having on Karen, who felt her face sink into an expression of misery.

Emma must have finally caught on and pressed ahead quickly. "I mean it's fine to go around to a pub for a pint with your friends, of course. And you're okay cause I'm here now."

"Thanks for saving me from myself," Karen said dryly.

"No worries. I'm in here every day anyway," said Emma, giving the bartender a scandalous grin.

Karen smiled into her glass despite herself. Emma's energy and choice of words never failed to entertain her. It livened up the library to no end. "What are you doing here?"

"Staff meeting today," Emma explained, as she fumbled with some bills in her wallet. "I've learned to never show up sober. So, what are you on about then?"

"Sorry?" Karen asked, not quite understanding the question.

Emma waved her hands about a bit. "You know, all this 'end of the world' gloominess you've got going on all the time. Depressing everyone left and right."

"Ahh," said Karen. "You're referring to my life."

"Yeah, that." Emma's attention was on the menu chalked on the wall. "Hang on a sec, will you? I'm starving." She headed toward the kitchen to order. "Want anything?"

Karen found that she was starving too. Apparently, you couldn't survive on Guinness alone. "Shepherd's pie, please."

Emma came back some time later laden with two steaming plates of food and two fresh glasses. Karen pulled her gaze from watching the murky shadows shift upon the floor and eagerly sniffed her pie.

"So," said Emma, shoving her fork into her own pie, "tell me all about it."

Karen took a long pull of her drink and told her the whole story. Every detail. Well, almost.

When Karen finished, she found Emma staring at her, an angry expression on her face.

"Why do you still wear that thing then?" She gestured at Karen's engagement ring.

Karen held out her hand, looking at the object in question as if examining a very stale biscuit. It was tiny, really. A thin band of gold with a speck of diamond stuck on three little prongs.

"It's part of me I guess . . . I know it sounds silly. It reminds me—"

"Of him?" Emma asked. "Don't you think you would be better off forgetting about it and moving on?"

Karen paused, attempting to summon her patience . . . and her dignity. "It's to remind me that marriage is an institution that you should never go into for the wrong reasons. It reminds me that I made a mistake—one that I shall never do lightly again.

"When Michael and I . . . that is, the first time—when we—" Karen coughed. "I lost my cross that day. I think it must still be there down by the creek. My mother gave me that silver cross when I was sixteen. I wore it every day. Soon after I lost the cross, Michael gave me my engagement ring. I think I associate the two. It's all I have left. I never got a wedding ring. We were short on money. And time."

"How did he propose?"

Karen closed her eyes, trying to recall the day, the scents, Michael's young face. Remembering when life seemed new. She opened her eyes and smiled. "He surprised me. I'll give him that much."

"Well?"

"I guess it started with my older brother Joe. Joe was always doing crazy things—science things. He was really into astronomy and the weather and nature. He kept a garden out in the woods so the other kids wouldn't ruin it. He grew everything from roses to rutabagas. I was only seven or eight, but he used to take me out there right before they would blossom. We would camp out in our little tent and some blankets and wait for the sun to come up and watch them bloom. Sometimes we would keep coming back for several days before they would open their petals for the first time."

52

"Slow town," remarked Emma.

Karen sipped lightly from her drink, her eyes twinkling despite the dim light of the pub. "He had this special breed of morning glories that he used to grow. They were pinkish white with little flecks of red. I remember the name: *Ipomoea*. I used to think even the name sounded wonderful. He used to get so excited. I know things always seem brighter and better when you look back to your childhood, but I still think that they were the most beautiful flowers I've ever seen."

Karen swept some of the gravy up with a forkful of mashed potatoes, absorbed in the resulting patterns as the brown fluid seeped about the plate. "Anyway, I think it was about three months after Michael and I—after, well, you know. One night our parents decided that we would be married in one month. No shotguns, fortunately. I still remember that night. Better than any other night in my life . . . almost.

"I made Michael come over to my house to talk and we went into the back yard. Joe was—Joe was gone, and he wasn't coming back. Gone to war. He left when I was still young. But he left the garden in my care. And every spring, I'd plant one of the seeds for Joe. Sentimental, I guess, but that's me all over.

"I knew it was about to bloom, you see, and I'd been telling Michael about it all week, so I called him over to watch. Our lives as we knew it were over. Or at least our youth. We stayed up all night talking about what we thought it would be like to be married. I don't really remember what we said that night. It would be interesting to remember. Eventually we ran out of things to say and just sat wrapped in Mama's quilt on the porch staring at the stars.

"We watched the sun come up together that morning. You know, I think I could count on my fingers the number of times that I have seen the sunrise. To see the dark blue fade into lighter and lighter shades as the rays of light push back the night and snuff out the stars—the purples, the golds, the clouds. Happens every day. And yet, every day I sleep right through it." Karen gave her head a little sad shake.

"We could see the touch of dew condense upon the grass." Karen continued. "It soaked right through my socks. I remember that now, when I walked to where I had planted Joe's Glory, although I don't think I noticed it then. Michael followed behind me. We sat in the grass and waited for it to open. We needed some sign of hope that day.

"It must have taken a half an hour, in reality. In my mind, it happened in seconds. The dew slid together and formed silver drops. As it unfurled, the water slithered off the silky petals as the flower opened for the rising sun. And inside something sparkled. I grabbed the flower so hard that bramble thorns went straight through my fingers. I plucked the ring up and spun around to find Michael kneeling in my radishes."

Karen looked up to find Emma staring at her, her mouth hanging wide open.

"I have never heard you talk like that," Emma said. "That's incredible. How did he—"

"Slipped it in the flower that night with a razor blade when he was quote, going to the bathroom, unquote."

"That's pretty impressive."

"Yes," agreed Karen, placing her silverware on the plate. "I'll give him some credit. When he wants to, Michael can be quite dazzling . . ." She trailed off, her eyes gazing into the middle distance. "Which is, of course, the problem. Mind you, the flower died the next day, a result of his razor work."

"Still," Emma protested. "Sounded good though." She glanced at her watch. "Come on, Mavis will start barking if we're late." She gathered up her purse and looked pointedly at Karen. "You are coming, aren't you?"

Karen grunted her acquiescence as she grabbed her own handbag. "I suppose. Work will help me keep my mind off it."

"You want my opinion?" offered Emma as she held the door open, letting in the glaring brightness of the outside world.

Karen squinted at her. She knew she didn't have to ask. Not with Emma.

"If I were you, I'd start doing some intensive research on mammoths!"

Chapter 12

With a vicious snap, Karen switched off the tape deck that was softly playing "Look Away" by Chicago. She leaned heavily on the desk and cradled her head in her hands. "Patrick, I think I'm in trouble."

Patrick looked up from the cart he was loading with books. "Why?"

"All these sappy songs, which I know are utter rubbish and have always thought were utter rubbish are actually starting to seem deep and meaningful," she said, idly staring at the occupants of the library. The usual odd assortment of people dotted the place: an old couple were reading a newspaper at one of the couches and a young blond woman, probably a student, was flipping through some magazines at a table while in the far corner. Mrs. Barnaby, the village babysitter read *Goodnight Moon* to her four charges. Two of the little kids were listening to the story while another played space shuttle with a biplane and a sock monkey. The fourth child had lodged herself within a low shelf empty of books and had fallen asleep, her long, golden hair dangling to the ground.

A positively bustling Wednesday night in Little Ivory's Public Library.

Karen mentally wished them all away. She still hadn't worked out why Michael was back . . . Or what to wear for her date on Friday with Eric for that matter.

She noticed that Patrick had vanished with his cart off into the stacks somewhere, leaving her alone behind the checkout desk. She wandered over to her little desk, plopped down and stared at the computer. The bluish screen glowed back at her, displaying the spreadsheet containing the data for the year's book purchases to date.

Karen glanced up at the clock and saw that it was only seven. The day had been a blur. Even the weekly staff meeting had seemed to take a few minutes. Mavis had even agreed to host the dance, so long as any profit would go to her large-print book program. But now there was still an hour to close, and the last thing Karen wanted to do was add and subtract, let alone contemplate how little money the library had left.

Depressing thoughts, after all, only led to more depressing thoughts. And Karen's primary goal of Day Three of Life (version 2.0) was to avoid such thoughts altogether.

She shunted away the spreadsheet and brought up a text program and began idly typing up a guest list for the dance. She had called up Oscar about his band, but his saxophone player had developed a severe heart condition since Christmas, so instead she had called up the Marples of La Grande Poisson and found that their little jazz quartet was free after nine o'clock and could play for a small fee. Karen booked the group, deciding that an admission fee must be asked after all. As she pondered the amount, she cleared the page of names—she knew who would come anyway, so it seemed silly to invite them—and, having settled on a four-dollar cover charge, she started typing up a poster instead.

Karen nearly finished after a few minutes but couldn't think of a catchy name for the dance. "Karen's Ball" didn't really sound quite right, nor did "Alzheimer's Waltz." She bandied about the name "Swing Out Loud," but that didn't ring true either. With a sigh, she saved the file and decided to clear her head. She brought up a new file and started tapping playfully at the keys:

Life sucks old furball weeds xxxxxx lkjalksdjf penguins and tacos and greennn

Karen glanced up from her screen to discover it was only quarter after seven and no one was looking like they wanted to check anything out yet. Patrick still hadn't reappeared, which was odd, as he was usually his most irritating in the evening when he had her as a captive audience. Karen's gaze wandered to the nearby Romance Fiction rack. She hadn't picked one up all day; been too busy, she reflected.

Who needs to read it when you're living it?

She stared at the blank screen.

Why not?

How hard could it be?

Slowly at first, she began to type.

~ φ ~

There was a little house that sat beside a creek. In the heat of summer, plants drooped and sagged until the tree boughs touched

56

the roof. There was a little wooden fence that encircled the house, but it couldn't keep the daughters inside where it was safe.

Nor could it keep out the boys.

~ φ ~

Karen stared at what she had written for a moment before toggling the *"Delete"* key. Too dark, she decided. She flexed her fingers dramatically and began again.

~ φ ~

The young maiden flew out of the house, her eyes brimming with tears, her chestnut hair streaming out behind her. She ran along the road under a canopy of thick leafy maples, her feet kicking up poofs of dust upon the dirt road. The young woman slowed as exhaustion replaced her anger. Checking her pace to a petulant stroll, she idly kicked at pebbles beside the road. She pulled her hair back and wiped the tears from her cheeks, looking rather smashing as she did so, dressed in a lovely white and blue skirt and a pair of terrific blue shoes that her mother had given her last Christmas.

It was ~~Karen's~~-Christina's favorite outfit.

The outfit her sister had just tried to steal out of her closet.

Which was the reason why Christina had run out of the house: to get away. To get away from her sister and her grabby hands, to get away from her mother and her worrying, and to get away from her father and, well, to get away from her father in general.

So, Christina ran, and when she couldn't run any farther, she walked. She soon found herself in a clearing by the footbridge that spanned Ebony Creek. She tossed herself down beneath a large oak tree and stared up at the sky.

It was during one of these sulks that she saw him. Mike Whittington was walking from his house, headed down the road toward her. She'd had a crush on him for two years straight, ever since he had taken her and her sister to the social that past summer. Christina quickly primped and preened to make sure that everything was in its best and most prominent position, rubbing the tears off her cheeks with the backs of her hands.

Mike had on a pair of white chinos and a plaid shirt, his hair gelled up. He hadn't noticed her yet.

"Mike," she called out.

He appeared lost in thought, looking at his feet as he walked, but he started at the sound of his name. He shaded his eyes from the blistering afternoon sun and spied Christina sitting among the trees and changed paths.

"What are you doing?" He stepped closer into the shade of the oak.

"Trying to get away from my family. What are you doing out? I thought you had practice."

"Umm, no not today, I . . . needed some fresh air. It's such a nice day," Mike explained quickly. He leaned closer as his eyes adjusted to the light and became aware of her pink cheeks and red eyes. He knelt beside her. "Are you okay?"

Christina looked up into his brown eyes, feeling her heart beat harder as he leaned closer. She took a quick, nervous breath. "It's nothing. Just family."

"I know how you feel." Mike sat beside her and pulled a blade of grass from the ground and started twisting it with his fingers. "My dad's drunk again. I had to get out of there."

"Oh, Mike," Christina put a kind hand on his shoulder. "I'm sorry."

"S'okay," he stared at the ground. "Family's what you got, right?" His fingers pulled a small stone out of the ground and flicked it into the creek, his eyes reflecting the waves that glinted in the afternoon sunlight. "Just gotta deal with it."

"I suppose." Christina absently stroked the silver cross that hung from her neck. "Sometimes I wish I could just run away, so far away they could never bring me back."

Mike grunted. "Where would you go?"

"I'm not sure," she said quietly. "But I've always wanted to go to Tonga."

"Tonga?" snorted Mike. "Where's that?"

"I don't know," said Christina, "but that's why, don't you see? How could they find me if they don't know where it is?"

"Two words for you," Mike said, a wicked smile on his face. "Rand McNally."

Christina frowned. "Are you going to offer to walk me home or not?"

"Sure," said Mike rising. He held out his hand to her. "I was just on my way to see—"

58

His foot got tangled in a root. As he fell, he twisted into her and they ended up as a pile of wayward limbs, spinning down the embankment toward the water.

Christina let out a little yelp of glee as they spun, laughing and rolling at the same time. At the last moment, she spread her arms wide to stop their tumble, pressing her palms into the ground. Mike rolled on top of her, his hands clasping hers to steady himself.

Their faces were inches apart.

Christina felt his chest heaving against hers as he fought to control his breath, could feel the sweat that clung to his palms as they clasped against hers, the weight of his body pressed against her.

Mike pulled away slightly, placing his hands on the ground by either side of her neck, raising his face above hers, his eyes wide, perhaps with indecision?

The rippling of the creek roared in her ears as he kissed her, long ago on that sunny day by the footbridge.

And he knocked her up with twins.

~ φ ~

Karen looked up from her screen as she heard Mrs. Barnaby gathering up the children and herding them to the door. Karen gave her a little wave as they left and then saw that it was ten to eight already. She walked up to the front desk and called out: "Closing time! The library will close in ten minutes!"

She watched in satisfaction as first the young blond woman left, closely followed by the old couple. Karen switched off the copier, returned the newspaper sticks to their rack, and logged out of the circulation system. She fiddled and fussed and generally tidied up the counters as the grandfather clock behind her ticked out the seconds remaining in the day.

She came back to her desk and stared at what was written. Okay, one anachronism at least and that last line would have to go, but still, she considered, not too horrible, but would it be filed under Fiction or Nonfiction? She paused for a moment. Once again, the fact that her life resembled a romance novel was slightly worrying.

But it was all true—well, mostly true, she corrected. From a certain point of view.

So sayeth Obi-wan Kenobi.

As she saved her story to a disk, she saw the Interlibrary Loan list and she swore under her breath. She had meant to pull the books off the shelves but had put it off all evening.

Oh, well, she thought, it's either tonight or tomorrow morning, and I'd much rather sleep in. She grabbed the list and ventured into the stacks.

Karen had already found two of the books before she made it into the P's. E. Peters, she paused, now is that Ellis or Emily? She crouched lower to make out the individual titles on the spines, trying to match it to the one on her list.

Clump. *Murder at the Chapel* jumped in her hand.

Clump. *Death Tolls Now* flew up at her face.

She jumped back as she heard the **clump** again, nearly falling against the stacks as a whole section of the shelf in front of her launched into the air. As books spilled around her legs, she heard the wet sounds of crying from the other side of the shelving. Worried, she waded through the books and peered around the other side of the stack.

Patrick was sitting on the floor, methodically kicking books off the shelves, harder and harder, tears streaming down his puffed, red face as he kicked and kicked, his hands clenched into little fists.

Kneeling beside him, Karen put a hand on his legs, but he kicked her away in irritation.

So, she sat next to him and waited.

After a few more kicks, there were no more books left on any nearby shelves, but he still kicked feebly at the empty air a few more times. Eventually, his energy spent, he stopped, staring up at the stacks that towered above them.

He rubbed the back of his hand across his nose and sniffed.

Karen waited.

"She wanted to see the sea." Patrick gnawed at his knuckles. His voice was dry and husky. "She wanted to go to one of those colleges with a semester at sea program . . . just wanted to see the Mediterranean." His words caught in his throat as if there was something inside threatening to boil out if he didn't let it.

Karen gently pulled his hand away from his mouth. He turned to look at her, as if realizing for the first time that she was there.

60

His eyes were bright red, the brown irises smoldering in the puffy pink skin that swelled around them.

"Who, Pat?" She asked quietly. "Who wanted to go to the sea?"

Patrick turned back to look up at the ceiling. "Sara," he whispered to himself.

"Sara?" asked Karen. The name sounded vaguely familiar, but she was none the wiser.

Patrick remained silent for nearly a minute before answering in a hushed voice, "Sara's dead."

Karen couldn't think of anything to say; her throat felt dry. Something spiky and painful had lodged there and she couldn't seem to breathe.

"She was crossing the street and her backpack broke open," Patrick went on in a flat monotone. "She bent down to pick up the books and they were all over the place and the guy didn't see her and she was only fourteen. She was only my age. We had English class together. She once told me she wanted to go to see the ocean, but her dad said they couldn't go last year cause they didn't have the money and they were going to go this year and all she wanted was to see and she was only fourteen and she's dead and she's dead and now she's . . ." and then Karen was holding him as he buried his face into her chest. She rocked him back and forth as he cried, stroking his head as he heaved and fought for his breath.

Karen realized that she was crying too, thinking of that fresh little library card she had pulled out reading the obituaries: Sara Millington had died in a car accident on Saturday. She remembered now. Unable to think of anything to say that could make Patrick feel better, she kept rocking him back and forth.

For a long time, all that could be heard among the stacks in the vast chambers of the library was the gentle sounds of sobbing.

Eventually, Karen found that her eyes hurt too much to cry anymore. She pulled out a couple of clean tissues from her pockets and she gave one to Patrick. As he accepted it, he seemed to realize how close he was to her and pulled away, scrunching back until he was sitting on the floor opposite, leaning against the now empty shelves.

It was about then that they realized that they were blowing their noses at each other and their sobbing was replaced by light, tired laughter as they took in their red noses and honking noises.

But it didn't last.

"Why?" Patrick asked after a long, awkward moment.

"What why?" Karen asked.

"What's it for?"

"Pat, you're only sixteen years old. You're not supposed to know the answers to the Meaning of Life," Karen admonished. "And don't look at me with those puppy eyes. I'm over fifty and I haven't figured out a damn thing."

"She never did anything wrong, she never hurt anyone." Patrick's ruby face crunched into a puzzled frown of pained innocence.

His expression was so beautiful in its honesty that it hurt her soul to look at it.

Karen suddenly had a vision of him much older, as a man with a dark expression cast over his visage after a lifetime of bitterness and prejudices battering this beautiful face. She found that she was softly crying again, not for Sara but for Patrick, who was still young and sitting across from her.

Patrick hadn't noticed. He was staring at the floor and rubbing his sore nose. "I keep thinking that if only I had talked to her a few minutes more at lunch she wouldn't have been in front of that car and she wouldn't have died but I didn't and now she's dead . . . And I'm not."

"Patrick." Karen gently dabbed at her nose. "Take it from someone who may be, according to some, old and not exactly wise, but take it from me that this is the first If in your life of a very large list of If's. None of them are easy and many . . . many hurt, but you can't change most of them." She tried to explain, but the words seemed to be hitting too close to home. She felt a cold, nauseous grip tighten around her heart. "I guess you just have to live life as best as you can and hope that you're happy and . . . and know it could end at any time."

Patrick sniffed.

"Well, it isn't Socrates," she admitted. "And it will probably make you a surly teenager ahead of schedule, but it's the only answer I have for you."

Karen stared off into the middle of the R's, lost in a world of her own.

"Dying seems easy," muttered Karen as dark thoughts roiled in her mind. "Sometimes I think it's living that scares me the most." She shook herself. "Now go on, you're not getting paid for this you know. It's after eight."

"Sorry about all this." Patrick looked at the books that lay strewn across the floor.

"That's okay." Karen spied a Tim Robin's book and gave it a hefty kick. It flew through the air to land atop the others. "I've been dying to do that for years. I'll take care of this. Go home. You need some rest."

Patrick struggled to his feet and headed for the back exit.

"Patrick—" Karen broke off as she realized that she didn't know what to say. She stumbled on anyway. "I hope . . . I hope it helped."

Patrick walked over until he was standing over her, looking down at her face.

For a moment, she feared he was going to hug her. Instead, he handed her back a soaked gob of tissues. He gave a sad smile then walked away, headed for the back door.

Well, one good deed for the day anyway.

Karen pulled herself up onto her knees and began re-shelving the books. Most of them were still in a sort of order, if lumped into clumps. As she placed one book after another on the shelves, she caught herself.

I've been so wrapped up in my own petty troubles that I didn't even know who Sara was.

A chill gripped her. Am I so obsessed with myself? That little pep talk I just gave to Patrick would have carried a little more weight if I hadn't been wallowing in self-pity for so long over an "If" of my own.

"Who was it that said that Irony was the fifth Force in the Universe?" she asked aloud.

"I think it was Ovid, but I could be wrong," answered a familiar male voice.

Karen dropped *Death by a Tabernacle* in shock as she spun around to find a man standing at the end of the stack.

Eric.

"Let me give you a hand." He knelt beside her and helped manhandle the remainder of the books on the shelves. They stood a few feet apart, caught in a moment of awkwardness.

"I was just, ah, straightening…" began Karen. His body filled the narrow space between the stacks, and she felt claustrophobic in the best possible way.

"I know," Eric nodded gently. "I overheard most of it."

"Oh." She noticed that he was wearing the same spicy cologne he had worn in graduate school.

"It was very kind," he said with a little smile. "I came here to pick up . . . well, the front doors were open. It's only eight. I didn't realize you closed so early."

Karen nodded. Eric had apparently forgotten that Little Ivory didn't work like the rest of the world; doors had locks, but they were rarely ever used. "The only door that locks in this place is the fire door, cause if it opens the alarm goes off and you can't have an alarm blaring away when people are trying to read, can you? Besides, the sprinkler went off once by accident and if it's one thing you don't want in a library filled with thousands of books is water soaking everything. They swell up in water, like some sort of strange sea creature . . ."

Karen was amazed that she had said all that in one breath. The bemused expression on Eric's face seemed to support this theory.

"I'm sorry," she blushed. "It has been a trying few days."

Eric smiled again, with that kind expression that made Karen feel all gooey inside.

"I should have realized you worked here," he went on. "I suppose I should have guessed."

"Job options for librarians can be a bit limited," Karen said, turning his words over in her head. Obviously, you're not here to see me . . . "Are you here for a book? Is there anything I can help you find?"

"No, that's all right. I came here to . . . I'll get what I need later—" He broke off and stared at her, concern evident in his eyes. "Did he hurt you?"

Karen looked down at herself in bewilderment. She noticed that the wounds inflicted by a panicked Mr. Hobbes had reopened, causing red streaks on the inside of her white shirtsleeves. She fumbled in one of her pockets for the bandages that she had been carrying about for the past twenty-four hours or so. "This wasn't Patrick, it's my wretched cat."

"Here, let me help you with that." Eric took her hand and guided her toward one of the reading tables. Gently peeling back her shirtsleeves, he unwrapped the old bandage with weathered, brown hands. Strong hands that had seen the dust and sunlight of a thousand days in other places, other times.

Hands that Karen found herself wanting to have touch her once more. She suddenly realized that they were.

Eric winced as he spied the red and white flesh that lay beneath the cotton. Claw marks cross-hatched her skin, evidence of Mr. Hobbes' harrowing escape from the bathtub.

"It's not as bad as it looks," said Karen as she saw his expression.

Eric carefully teased away small bits of cotton that had healed into the wound.

Karen flinched.

"A bit like life, isn't it?" He reached for a new bandage but kept one hand resting on her arm.

As she stared at Eric's hand, the English language suddenly seemed too complex and foreign for Karen's tongue to grasp. After an eternity, she managed to find her voice. "What do you mean?"

"This." He gestured at her wound. "Life can hurt, but it's not half as bad as it looks sometimes." Seeing her perplexed expression, he expounded. "I heard the last part of what you were saying to that young man."

"It can certainly scar sometimes." Karen nodded, glad of the distraction from the pain. She watched him, transfixed as he unrolled the fabric and started re-binding her wound. She missed those shoulders.

"But the body forgets pain, doesn't it?" he continued.

Karen thought of the birth pains that she had with Jim and Tommy, the searing, ripping, blinding . . . Words could describe it, but her mind had forgotten the actual sensations. "Yes . . ." she said slowly.

"Sometimes the only way to know that you're truly alive is if you get hurt. Even just a little. Don't you think?"

Karen considered. "I'd rather not get hurt in the first place."

"Ah, but the only way to avoid getting hurt is to not do anything," he pointed out, his voice almost a whisper. "And doing nothing, well, it isn't living. Is it?"

"It's a risk, I suppose," agreed Karen.

He finished re-dressing her bandage and looked up at her, his eyes peering out from beneath his bushel of hair. He flashed another fabulous smile at her. "At least you'll have the scars to prove it."

Yes, it proves I was stupid enough to let my cat in the bath. I'll have it engraved on my tombstone.

He stood up and made to leave through the main doors.

"Wait," said Karen, fumbling to rise and follow him. "We're still on for Friday, aren't we?"

"Of course," he said as he turned back to the door. "Till Friday then."

~ φ ~

Karen didn't remember much of the rest of the night. She threw the fallen books haphazardly back on the shelves and raced home. She picked up the phone six times before deciding that she had pestered Claire enough lately. She settled on telling the whole story to Mr. Hobbes several times.

She finally started some loads of laundry to keep her thoughts focused on reality. On her third load, she spied the answering machine light blinking determinedly. She toggled the play button with an elbow as she passed, a full basket of undies in her arms. She dumped the load on her bed and began sorting as she listened to the scratchy message.

"Karen, this is Mavis. I was just calling about our library dance this Friday—"

"Our?" Karen parroted in outrage, flinging a panty at a sleeping Mr. Hobbes.

"—and, well, it's just that my brother moved to town last weekend and I know that you don't have a date—"

The squawk, when it came, was loud enough to flatten Mr. Hobbes' ears against his skull. Fortunately, it served as a warning that enabled him to dodge the airborne laundry basket.

Karen punched the *"Delete"* button with her fist and swore.

"I know you don't have a date . . . you utter bitch!" she yelled at the machine. She kept swearing until she felt slightly better. It

66

was only then that she discovered Mr. Hobbes ensconced in the warm pile of freshly laundered clothes, blessing them with a thin layer of cat hair.

Karen decided to call it a night. She was half-tempted to make some popcorn and dine on cake, but didn't really feel up to the aftereffects, no matter how good the dream might be. She stared at the printout of the poster that she had dashed off at work and lay on her bed wondering what Friday might be like.

THE

SECOND CHANCE DANCE

IVORY PUBLIC LIBRARY

FRIDAY, 8:00 P.M.

FABULOUS FORTIES FLING

MATURE MEMBERS ONLY

Chapter 13

File, index, sort.
File, index, sort.
File, index . . .

The hours passed slowly, the drudgery of work imposing a structure on her otherwise chaotic week. It had started as one of those mornings when she wanted nothing more than to snuggle under her warm blankets, bury her nose into the pillow, and go back to sleep.

Unfortunately, it was Karen's day to open the library. So, she had dragged herself out of bed, crawled to the shower, and gulped down some coffee.

She had work to do.

She rolled in the books from the outside drop box, booted up the circulation system, and prepped the desk. She had a quick chat with Mr. Thornton, their maintenance man, about getting those new squishy cinnamon buns for the vending machine in the lobby, before switching on all the lights and throwing open the doors to the outside world.

Only a few people trickled in that morning. Mr. Oates came in for the daily crossword. Mrs. Wilson brought her toddlers in to play with the cardboard books and puzzles while she sorted through the help-wanted ads. Emma came in for a quick meeting with Elsa before they both vanished to their respective back offices. Karen used the time to make copies of her dance poster. She finished the interlibrary loan requests and straightened a few shelves before taking up her position behind the front desk.

Karen found that if she kept working, she could avoid thinking about—certain things that she didn't want to think about. She toddled over to Mavis' station and mucked about in its vast piles of papers until she found the forms for ordering new books for the library. She grabbed the book catalogue from beneath the potted azaleas, arranged herself at the desk, and started selecting new titles to order.

At noon, Karen took a break and made a fresh cup of cocoa. While cautiously sipping her mug, she scanned the book titles she had scribbled down: twelve self-help books on relationships, six dealing with aging, two on cat health, and one copy of *Quotable Shakespeare*.

With a sigh, she crumbled up the list and tossed it in the recycle bin.

She padded over to the computer and started hunting and pecking at the keys. She had to make a new sign for the library; they were closing early to attend Sara's funeral. As she typed, she found that even work could no longer distract her. She sat in a daze, wondering how time could pass so slowly and how life could be so intolerably cruel, until it was time to shut down the library.

~ φ ~

The smell of roasting almonds and the sweet bite of mocha steeped the air and steamed up the window panes. With her hands clasped firmly around the tall cup, Karen breathed in the rich flavor of her Irish coffee. The summer student crowd was randomly dotted around her like nuts fallen in the shade of a tree. They roosted at small circular tables, pretending to be studying but their eyes were constantly peering at each other and flicking to the door alert for new arrivals. They hadn't spared Karen more than a passing glance.

Which was exactly why Karen liked to come and read at the Black Forest Café. She didn't exist here. No one bothered her. It was just her coffee and a few books.

Watching the wisps of steam spiral up from the foamy skin of her Irish coffee, Karen knew she wasn't fooling anyone. She was stalling. The texture of the Styrofoam cup felt dry and rubbery against her skin. The wake was in two hours and by all rights she should be at home getting ready. But she knew she wasn't ready to face it just yet, although it wouldn't do to see the Reverend while liquored up.

Karen picked up *Love and Treachery in the Darkness of the Subcontinent* and carefully turned to the marked page. Usually, she could devour a novel in an hour, two tops, but the character of Katherine Stone held a special place close to her heart. Even starting this next chapter was violating her usual rule of one a week in an attempt to make the novel last as long as possible. The six-month wait until the next novel was released was always too much to bear.

Unfortunately, Karen was learning how quickly those months and years could slip from her grasp. She needed reassurance that somewhere out there, the right thing was being done and that there was still good in the world. It seemed lately that only Professor Katherine Stone could provide that . . .

~ φ ~

Katherine threw down her gear and peered through a gap in the rocks at the boulder-strewn landscape. She had made it at last! She folded up the tattered map and carefully stowed it in her satchel. Pulling out her compass, she took readings to confirm their destination.

Logan kneeled beside her, refilling his bottle from the stream that ran beside them. Lost in thought, Kate watched him wash his face, her eyes lingering on the crystal droplets that dripped from his stubbly chin.

Carefully making note of the direction in her notebook, she turned to the final page to examine the final clue her father had left embedded in the Cobra Codex:

'Serpent's Skin and Teeth of Glass Will Reveal the Crystal Path'

According to Logan, this last puzzle would reveal the location of the entrance to the Caves of Alexander, but try as she might, the clue had eluded her for weeks. Her thoughts drifted once again to Logan. His thick shoulders atop his slender waist were a distraction. He dipped his strong forearms into the stream, cupping water in his hands before using his sensuous lips to drink deeply. The metallic gray rock wall behind him emphasized his chestnut hair slicked back by the—

"Serpentinite!" She nearly leapt into the air with excitement.

Logan almost fell into the stream. "What?"

Kate pointed to the rock surface across the stream. "That's it! Serpentinite, a metamorphic rock, see?" She splashed gaily into the stream. When she reached the rock wall, she ran her hands across the surface that shimmered in muted purples, greens, and blues of slanted crystals. The colors ran in slithering stripes that undulated across the face of the boulder and wrapped around to disappear along the cliff edge. "The skin of the serpent! The final clue! We just have to follow the formation to the caves!"

Kate felt Logan's hand caress her neck, but she never felt the pain of her head slamming into the rock. She saw nothing but a blinding white as she slipped from consciousness.

~ φ ~

"You know, if you ever get sick of those, I think you could get a bottle of wine for the same price."

A pot-bellied bundle of denim flopped down in the chair across from her. Karen grumbled a bit as she put down her book. "Hello, Mark."

She needed a t-shirt that read: Leave me alone, I'm reading.

Mark was not by profession a psychic, but he appeared to have read the expression on Karen's face. He raised his hands to placate her. "Not here to bug you, honest." Scratching the tuft of brown hair that clung to the side of his balding head, Karen saw that for the first time that she had known him, he looked exhausted.

Whenever his name was mentioned, she remembered the image of him with Claire at their wedding, beaming proud and full of hope. Today, however, his dark skin was stretched tight across his face. He rubbed his chin with a hand nervously. "School was only half day today, we let our prisoners go early so that they could attend, well, you know."

It only occurred to Karen at that point that Mark had known Sara personally, that she had probably been in his science lessons. Karen let her disgruntled expression relax into one of compassion. She touched his arm in sympathy.

"Never understood it myself." He gestured at her paperback. "But I don't have much time to read anything these days."

As innocuous as his comment was, Karen found herself on the defensive. The topic was familiar, and better yet, completely removed from what was really on her mind. "Some of them are quite well-written and researched." Karen pulled the book closer to her. "And, despite the covers, most of them are very empowering."

Mark peered at the cover in question: a tall busty woman with a peculiar marking on her shoulder was fighting off some improbable looking natives, and two dark, flexing men were shackled to a wall behind her. "My mother used to observe that while the other kids were out doing things under bridges and at parties, I'd be in my room reading Bronte. She used to say that reading was my drug. My escape. Of course, it appears as if I've been reading the wrong works. I'd love to be empowered by her."

Karen rolled her eyes and turned the book over, face down on the table. As she did so, she found herself grateful for Mark providing the distraction. From the look in his eyes, she realized that even though his hurt was much deeper than hers, he was still trying to help ease her pain. It was one of those moments when Karen realized why Claire had married a man with such a peculiar nose. "Is there a reason you didn't become a psychologist?"

"Being a schoolteacher is being a psychologist." Mark stood up from the table and picked up his order from the counter. "Worse pay but better vacations." He held the door open for her. "You ready?"

"No," Karen replied as she gathered up her book and her cup. "No, I don't think I am."

Chapter 14

Sara was wearing a little white dress, trimmed with lace, and swathed in blue ribbon.

After leaving Mark, Karen had spent most of the afternoon running around town pinning up copies of her poster. First the post office, then museum, then Leon's Market and Jane's Tea Shoppe. Finally, of course, she put one up at the library.

Karen was driving back home when she passed Giorgio's Funeral Parlor and reconsidered, then went back around town, taking the posters down and stuffing them into the trunk of her car. Once home, Karen had spent another hideously long time in front of the mirror choosing the appropriate apparel for the funeral. The dressing on her wound needed changing, but she left the old bandage Eric dressed her with on for emotional support.

It was Sara's favorite dress, Karen later learned. There were still the teardrop stains where some grape juice had left a permanent mark. Lying atop the cotton of Sara's dress was a plain silver cross. One of the lights in the room reflected off the metal, creating a tiny haze of light.

Karen half-fancied she could see her mother's face reflected in the haze of that light, staring at her from Beyond. Just for a moment Karen thought she could see her, but she couldn't be sure.

Because everything was really blurry right now.

Karen couldn't stop her eyes from filling up with tears, no matter how many times she rubbed them with her handkerchief. She really wanted to see her own mother right now, because there was a girl who should have become a young woman in front of her wearing a little white dress that was just like the one she had when she was a kid and she wanted to tell her that she had one too, but she couldn't get the girl in front of her to wake up and it wasn't fair cause she had had a chance at life but she had messed everything up and she couldn't bring herself to look at Sara's face and it wasn't fair.

~ φ ~

Sara Millington was pronounced dead at St. Jude's Hospital at three twenty-five p.m. on Saturday afternoon due to internal hemorrhaging. The wake was held at Giorgio's Funeral Home at three p.m. on Thursday.

It rained at her funeral. No one seemed to notice. Around a tiny hole in the ground crowded over two hundred waxy black umbrellas. Karen stood a little apart from the crowd, just far enough away to hear James, the Reverend, give his spiel about life and death, but she didn't want to be too close to the grave. Karen finally remembered she had helped Sara at the library once find a couple of books on alligators a few years ago. A few years ago . . . and now Karen was standing by a hole in the ground so that they could hide this child in it.

She never even really knew Sara.

Perhaps that was the worst part of all.

Karen found herself listening to the incessant tapping of rain as it spattered against her umbrella, the Reverend's words drowned out by the random noise. She stared off into the sky, a flat gray wall that shrouded them all. Another freak of Little Ivory nature. It was sunny at Karen's house when she left but pouring in town. She had to scrabble in the car for an umbrella for the downpour that drenched the funeral procession.

As if the little town knew, somehow.

Karen suddenly found herself wanting something a lot stronger than Irish coffee.

~ φ ~

Leaning against the bonnet of her car, Karen watched the little congregation disperse as people slowly headed for home. Life seemed thick and slow compared to the racy events of the past few days.

"Are you okay?" asked a voice from behind her.

Karen turned to find Mavis peering out from beneath the awning of a huge umbrella. She almost didn't see Elsa huddled under the shadow beside her.

"I'm fine," barked Karen. Then she realized how harsh it must have sounded, so she added, "Thanks for asking."

"I'm sorry to bother you, but I was just thinking about this dance of yours," began Mavis.

Oh, it's suddenly "mine" now, is it? Karen tasted the bite of bile struggling to rise through the blanket of grief.

"It may not be the best time . . ."

For the first time that Karen could remember, she agreed with Mavis.

Suddenly the Earth did not open and swallow her up whole.

Karen felt a vague sense of disappointment but nodded. "It's not exactly tactful, is it? I was thinking the same thing myself. I've already taken down the posters."

"It's for the best, probably," Mavis sighed, turning to look at the freshly turned earth of the grave. "Perhaps in a few weeks."

"I don't think so at all," said Elsa quietly.

"What?" Mavis turned to stare at the little woman.

"You don't get it, do you?" A pained expression pulled at Elsa's mouth.

"Get what?" asked Karen.

Elsa flapped her arms around a bit as if searching for the right words, causing the umbrella to wobble. It was as if she were desperately trying to convey something that she felt was so simple, yet something that no one else seemed to understand.

"We need it. We need this dance." Elsa pouted. "Even more now because of this. Everybody does," she said pointedly to Karen, "not just you."

"It's rude," retorted Mavis sharply. "A girl has just died. How do you think her parents will feel if the town has a party when their daughter dies?"

"They're leaving tonight to go to stay with relatives in the city," explained Elsa.

"Are you saying that we should celebrate the fact that she's dead and we're not?" asked Karen.

"No," said Elsa. "We should celebrate the fact that we are alive."

"What's the difference?" asked Mavis.

"I guess you wouldn't know, would you?" Elsa looked at first Mavis then Karen, disgusted. "Either of you."

"What is that supposed to mean?" Mavis demanded.

"It means that you're too busy sticking yourself in other people's lives instead of actually getting one for yourself." Elsa's voice raised to a squeak. "If you bothered to take a look at what you laughingly call your own life, you'd see a lonely old lady with no real friends with a sad excuse for a job who everyone avoids. And you," she said, turning on Karen, wielding a finger like a hot poker, "you're so busy moping about how you've 'screwed up' your own life so badly that you've given up living the time you have left. Both of you have lived Sara's life several times over, yet you fail to realize that this is something rare and special and some people who are crippled, blind, or deaf would be thankful to have over and over. That's what you're supposed to celebrate!"

With that, Elsa stalked off into the rain, leaving Karen and Mavis looking at each other in amazement.

They watched the little figure retreat.

Karen shuffled from one foot to another and stared at a pebble by her foot, searching for something to say. Then she looked up at the trees, their leaves heavy with water. The forest green lamppost. The tombstones.

"There was a large psychological component to Elsa's degree at the Academy," explained Mavis after a while. "I read it on her resume."

Karen had found her voice once more. "Mine was anthropology, actually," she said in a small voice.

"So was mine."

Karen blinked at Mavis.

"What was your thesis area?" Mavis asked.

Karen found herself dealing unexpectedly well with this voice that was using Mavis' larynx; a voice that was neither condescending nor grating to the ear and contained information that was potentially interesting. She still had a few qualms with the body this strange voice inhabited, but Elsa's little outburst had struck a few chords. More like scraping a hacksaw across the strings of a Stradivarius than chords, really. The words had hurt much deeper than they should.

"Meso-Amerindian cultures," Karen answered. "What was yours?"

"Polynesian fertility rites."

Karen blinked again. Repeatedly. She couldn't help but ask, "Did you get to, er, conduct field research?"

"I spent three months one summer touring the isles, but then the grant money ran out. Not a lot of cash in anthropology." Mavis let out a sigh and spun the umbrella that rested on her shoulder, sending out a little spray of droplets. "Traveled the world twice over. And yet, somehow, we all end up back here."

"Yes," said Karen numbly as she watched Old Bill shovel the first spade of dirt into the grave. Grave. Funny word for such a tiny hole. "We all end up here."

~ φ ~

Mr. Hobbes was bored.

Servant-Woman had left early in the morning, negligent in her duties to make the Place of Food cool. As the sweltering heat of the afternoon pervaded Mr. Hobbes' home, he had been forced to leave, settling in a breezy patch of shadow beneath a large pine tree on the back lawn. He stretched out on the crunchy carpet of pine needles and spent the day napping. Every so often a sparrow would interrupt his sleep, swooping at him, diving out of the sky to skim at his head or tail. He had strategically placed himself near one of their nests purely for such entertainment.

Now, however, he was bored. He had slept almost enough for one afternoon and Servant-Woman was late in returning. With no fresh meat, he would be forced to dine on the stale flavored gravel that she left in his other bowl. He yawned in disgust and began to lick at his fur half-heartedly, however his tongue wasn't really into it. He stretched a bit before settling down for his later afternoon nap, resting his chin on a front paw and flicking his tail distractedly.

The sound of an approaching human reached him. His ears twitched into the alert position and his eyes snapped open. The human was approaching across the grass, but it did not have Servant-Woman's form. Mr. Hobbes' nostrils flared, obtaining a whiff of a scent on the summer breeze that identified the figure. Mr. Hobbes' ears flicked back in irritation: it was Fat-One, the Servant that he had dismissed many, many Sheddings past due to "the Incident."

The man didn't see him but continued to walk until he stood by the swing that dangled from the old oak tree. He paused for a moment, running a hand over the worn and tattered rope and across the gray, rain-battered boards. Cautiously, he lowered himself onto the swing and stared out across the abandoned farmland behind the house.

Mr. Hobbes detected no fragrance of aggression or hostility from the human yet remained wary. He pretended to ignore the man, feigning sleep. However, the human remained motionless and uninteresting. A silent statue, the man soon blended into the tapestry of his territory. Eventually, Mr. Hobbes fell asleep.

A new scent woke him up again. He snapped his head up, shaking it angrily; he had not heard her arrival. Servant-Woman was standing by an entrance to the Place of Food, glaring at the human male sitting on the swing. The man had his back to her, still staring off into the distance of the setting sun.

Mr. Hobbes caught a whiff of anger from Servant-Woman. His fur raised on end as he watched her stride across the lawn. A fight! His muscles tensed as he pulled himself into an attack position. He tucked his back legs under him, claws pressing into the ground for purchase, reveling in the adrenaline that raced through his little body. Something interesting at last!

Even as he readied himself, however, he caught a change of scent from Servant-Woman and her determined stride broke halfway across the lawn. She paused, her eyes fixed on the figure before her. Something inside the woman seemed to give. Her shoulders slumped slightly, and she relaxed her clenched hands.

When she resumed walking, her pace was slower, her figure lighter somehow, as if she had left something weighty behind. She seemed much older than Mr. Hobbes could remember. Old and worn.

Mr. Hobbes felt the fight energy drain from him as well. As he did so, he felt echoes of pain sting at his little muscles.

They were both old. Both tired.

Mr. Hobbes gave a little cat sigh, puzzled by the actions of his pets once more, and watched the couple as the evening slipped by.

~ φ ~

"Hi."

"Hi." Michael didn't turn around, staring off into the fields instead.

"I think I should say I'm sorry—" Karen began.

"That's okay—"

"But I'm not."

"Oh." Michael said quietly.

Silence.

Karen sat on the swing, pulling up her legs beneath her.

Michael handed her the flask he'd been drinking from. She gave it a whiff: brandy. She pulled a long sip, shuddering at the burning sensation as the fluid slipped down her throat.

He gave the ground a little kick and together they slowly rocked back and forth. "I never had a chance to ask . . ."

"What?" She looked up at him curiously.

"How are you?"

"Tired." Karen ran a finger along the scratchy rope as she took another sip of the liquor. "Very tired."

"Should I fear for my life?" Michael gave his nose a thoughtful rub.

"No, I think that I'm too tired for revenge anymore. Seems silly somehow. That's why, rationally, I should feel sorry for almost killing you . . ."

"Thanks."

". . . however, emotionally it's another thing. So, no I'm not sorry, but I think I'm done punishing you. Seems like a waste of time." She found she was too tired to restrain the question she had wanted to ask for days. "What are you doing here?"

"Felt homesick . . ."

This isn't your home.

"It was, once," he said, as if reading her thoughts. "We did have some good times."

"Yes," replied Karen. "Yes, we did."

"I came back to make things okay between us."

Silence.

Shoosh.
Creak.
Swoosh.
Swipe.

"I went to Sara's funeral today."

"I heard," said Michael quietly. "I would have gone, but I didn't know her, or her parents."

As they rocked back and forth, Karen found herself staring at her hands in her lap, toying with her ring.

80

"Usual sermon about butterflies and mysterious hands of God et cetera?"

"I got told off, actually."

"By the Reverend?" Michael asked, his eyes wide.

"No. I think I would have preferred that." Karen sighed heavily. "One gets used to the idea of eternal damnation after a while."

"You're not going to hell, Karen," Michael said, the beginnings of a smirk forming on his face.

"It was Elsa, of all people."

"Elsa?" Michael frowned. "The mousy blob with the wispy hair?"

"Not exactly very kind, but accurate." Karen took another pull of brandy. The flask was nearly empty.

"I didn't know she could talk."

"I think she surprised herself, as much as us."

"What did she say?"

Shoosh.
Creak.
Swoosh.
Swipe.

"That I've been wallowing in self-pity for the last decade and been ignoring the simple fact that I'm alive. Basically."

"And have you?"

"Yes. Although it's one of those hindsight things when actually you're living it."

"I suppose I should know why you've been wallowing for so long."

"You don't get three guesses."

"I'm sorry."

"Let's not start that again," said Karen wearily. "I should have been angry, I was angry, I have been angry . . ."

"Sounds like a very tense situation."

Karen winced at the pun. "Don't make me get out the cordless," she threatened. "The point is, I'm not any of those things anymore."

"All because of Elsa?"

"Yes. No . . . Maybe." Karen pursed her lips. "I think it was the whole funeral/tell-off combo."

"Double whammy?"

"It's probably a good thing, really. I suppose now I should go and grab life by the throat and live life to the fullest, yadda, yadda, yadda . . ." Karen pulled her feet up onto the seat and hugged her legs.

"But?" prompted Michael.

"I'm too tired to give a damn right now about anything."

The swing continued to rock. Evening was upon them now, and the hum of insects was winding down. Another day was ending.

How many more did they have left?

"So," began Michael. "Where do you go from here?"

Shoosh.
Creak.
Swoosh.
Pause.
Swipe.

"ARRRGGGHHHH!" shouted Michael, as he flew off the swing. Clutching his shin, he tried to remain standing, hopping in place on his good foot.

Karen steadied the swing and peered beneath the slats of the seat. Mr. Hobbes was sitting quietly on the grass, looking up at her with an adoring expression on his face, whiskers spread wide.

"God-damn little bastard!" Michael screamed.

Karen gave Mr. Hobbes a little wink, before rising to help Michael. He leaned on her shoulder to steady himself as he rubbed his wound. "You trained him to do that, didn't you?"

"He still hates you for getting him neutered."

"It was your idea!" Michael protested. "I'm just the one who took him to the vet!" He pulled his sock further up his leg so that it covered the slashes. He placed his foot back on the ground cautiously.

As he did so, Karen was suddenly aware that his arm was still wrapped around her shoulders. He cast an anxious glance at her face, his body poised to dodge a sudden blow.

Instead, Karen gave his hand a little pat and linked arms with him.

His eyebrows twitched in surprise.

Karen gave a little laugh. The first laugh in a very long day. "It's a beautiful evening; let's go for a walk. For old time's sake."

~ φ ~

They walked down the lane not sharing a word, listening to the sounds of the birds in the trees and taking deep breaths filled with the scents of the wood. They marveled at the colors that cascaded across the sky as the sun slipped behind the trees. Eventually, they came upon a cluster of aspen, their leaves trembling in the warm evening breeze. They lifted a crossbar of the fence that lined the lane and slipped through. Karen felt the same thrill shudder through her as she had felt all those years ago, when they had done this together before. The wonderful sense of doing something ever so slightly wrong but in the best possible sense of wrong. Of stepping beyond borders into the magical world of the unknown. Into the woods.

They slipped quietly along the path, each step becoming more familiar, each more certain as they wove through the oaks and maples. They trod carefully through the undergrowth, the whites and greens shifting to the secret silver and gray colors that the night cast across the forest floor. The buzz of insects faded into the chorus of the cheeping of frogs that swelled in the summer air.

Soon, the pair heard the roar of water ahead and mist dabbed playfully at their skin. The trees fell away, and they stepped into a clearing, a patch of grass just above the streambed, and the world unfolded around them. The creek chuckled quietly to itself as it swept away and meandered aimlessly into the darkness of the woods. In front of them a wall of rock rose out of the forest floor, soaring hundreds of feet to scrape the sky. Through the ceiling of mist, they could just make out tiny pinpricks of light as the first of the stars appeared in the night sky, millions of miles distant, winking playfully at them.

Atop the cliff above them, the stream slipped over the edge of the world and poured down toward them, its descent marked by a throaty laugh as the water danced down the cliff to bounce and splash into the pool at its feet. Behind the flickering and shifting wall of water, in an alcove set deep into a cliff of oil shale, a natural flame lit by some passing hiker blazed brightly. The sheen of the waterfall around the flame acted as a prism, causing the spray to shift and shimmer with all the colors of the rainbow.

Sitting on a moist patch of grass, it seemed as if they could soak up time from the world around them, snatching a few precious moments from beyond life. Moments that they shared once, long ago, that merged with the present and all that had passed in between seemed unreal in this thaumaturgical place. Their place in their time.

Karen leaned her head on his shoulder, her breathing in time with his, her mind empty of all those petty trifles of everyday life and thought of nothing but of just being. She thought of how wonderful it was that she could still feel the same way now as when she had been nothing more than a child. She realized in that moment that even if you can't relive the past, you could make the present even better.

She didn't know how long they sat like that. When he rose to his feet and she stared into his eyes, the stars behind him were ablaze. He pulled her to her feet, and they moved to the ledge above the pool. Fireflies weaved and bobbed along the shore, flashing coyly at their reflections in the water. Then, with a wicked smile on his face, he stepped into the curtain of the waterfall, his head upturned, and his arms spread wide as the droplets showered about him. His hair plastered to his forehead, and his white shirt became translucent and pink.

He reached out a hand for her.

Without pause for thought, Karen stepped into the spray, emitting a gasp as the cool water splashed against her face. The ledge was mossy and slick, and her foot slipped beneath her, her eyes catching a flash of the fire through the watery curtain—

didn't mean a thing . . . you said you loved me you bastard . . . we both know it has to end; it's not forever, but if it's not forever, then what's it for???

—but before she could fall, she felt his arm across her waist, pulling her back from the pool. She instinctively clasped her arms around him to steady herself. Righted, she felt a moment of awkwardness slap against her as she made slight jerking movements to pull away. Then she looked into his eyes, through the spray, alight from the flames, eyes she had spent fifteen years looking into—

Michael cried when Banya, their Labrador, died and she held him all night . . . Yes, I will marry you now stop kneeling in my radishes . . . I want to see eternity with you and grow old . . . Tommy, we'll call him Tommy after your father . . . are you going to just sit there sulking or are you going to kiss me?

And she slipped her arms around him once more, stepping slightly closer, her face upturned, feeling the water run across her face, her neck, soaking into her blouse and dress. The cold plucked at her skin, raising a million goose bumps. She pressed closer to him and when at last she opened her eyes again, his face was above hers, his head tilted, his lips parted, tentatively pressing closer but waiting for acceptance. She found herself leaning into him and her hands grasping his neck and pulled him to her. Their lips brushed gently, cold wet lips, quivering with something akin to fear. Then they pressed together again, their mouths were wide, their tongues sliding and searching, sharing their warmth amid the numbing spray.

As the fireflies chased and darted across the pool, the gas flames flickered brightly, silhouetting the couple embracing in the waterfall. They remained standing like that for a long time.

Chapter 15

Karen woke up next to Michael. She stared at the brown mound of flesh that was his shoulder. Two empty bottles of wine stood on the coffee table. Their clothes from last night, still damp, were draped on furniture throughout the living room. Her head ached. A bed sheet was draped across the two of them. Her memory of the previous night was a bit hazy, full of spilt merlot and laughing at old photographs.

Did she dream the waterfall? Did it even happen?

She was fairly certain, at least, that they hadn't had sex.

She stared at the photos splayed on the carpet. "Why?"

Michael let out a groan as he attempted to burrow his head into the poofy softness of a pillow. "What?" he asked sleepily.

"Why? Why did you marry me?" She turned away as he rolled over to face her.

"Because you were pregnant with Jim and Tommy. That's how it was in those days." His voice was weary with sadness. "We didn't know what we were doing. And I wouldn't leave until you were all able enough to take care of yourselves. I couldn't."

"I know that," Karen said, her voice scratchy and thick. "What I want to know is, how could you lie to me for so long?"

"Because I did love you," Michael said, and his tone suggested he was as surprised by his words as Karen was. Possibly. Probably not.

Karen found that she was biting her lip.

"I still do," he went on. "Do you think I could stay with someone for fifteen years that I didn't love? But I was with Beth first, before you. We, Beth and I, had—have something special, something different. A special love. With you and me, we grew to love, but I've always loved Beth."

This was making far too much sense. Karen's mind went back to the woods, all those years ago, as she ran down the lane in her new dress . . .

Mike pulled away slightly, placing his hands on the ground by either side of ~~Karen's~~ Christina's neck—pulled away, to get away

86

from her — *raising his face above hers, his eyes wide, perhaps with lust?*

Or indecision?

Karen closed her eyes and said the one thing that she had left to cling to, the one brick left in a wall of lies: "You knocked me up."

Christina frowned at him. "Are you going to offer to walk me home or not?"

"Sure," said Mike rising. He held out his hand to her. "I was just on my way to go see—"

Michael put a hand on her shoulder. "That's not how I remember that day and neither do you," he whispered.

. . . The new dress her sister had wanted to wear that night.

"—to see your sister."

Karen felt the tears sting her skin, and she was glad he couldn't see her face.

The rippling of the creek roared in her ears as their lips met— as *she* kissed him—*long ago on that sunny day by the footbridge.*

"Karen?"

"Karen? I came to talk to you about Beth."

. . . We had—have something special . . .

"Beth?" Karen asked, her voice hoarse and lifeless.

"Yes, she—"

Karen snapped her head up and swirled around to face him. She stared at him steadily, the look in her cold brown eyes cutting off his flow of words. She knew with certainty what he was going to say. But she asked anyway.

"You're still with her, aren't you?"

Michael nodded.

Karen sagged into her pillows and slowly closed her eyes.

Silent.

She was disgusted. She felt dirty. But disgusted with him, or herself?

Disgusted with Life, she decided.

Disgusted and too angry for words.

Count to ten, she told herself, as her hands clenched and scrunched the sheets up around her shoulders. Count and breathe. She listened to the sound of her heartbeat echoing against the pillow. Listened as the roaring throb beat out of proportion to her heart, like far-off thunder. Breathing deeply, she clutched and unclutched her pillow with her fingers.

Breathe.

Better. She could cope now. She was cooling off, soothed by the sound of her blood slowly gushing about, the sound of Mr. Hobbes' scraping at the litter box in the hall, the sound of her own breath, the sound of his breathing next to her, the feel of his leg brushing against her thigh as he shifted slightly . . .

What only moments before had felt comforting—even arousing—his warmth, his smell, his presence was now driving her into an insane rage.

Okay, she told herself, maybe we'll try for twenty seconds.

No good.

She unfolded her legs and slipped her feet onto the floor, tossing the covers back. She stood up, her back to him.

"Get out," she said softly.

"What?"

"Get OUT!" Her voice raged into a hoarse whisper. "Get out."

She walked to her bathroom door. She paused in the doorway.

"Karen—" he protested, sitting up in the bed.

"I'm going to take a shower now. When I come out, I want you to be gone."

"But—" he tried again.

"Just leave. Please. Just leave. Now." She closed the door behind her, shutting him out. She yanked the water on and pulled herself into the cold spray. "Just leave, just leave, just leave," she repeated over and over.

And when she opened the door again, he was gone.

Chapter 16

"Here you go." Emma dropped the file on Karen's desk accompanied by a hearty thud. "Last month's invoices."

Karen peered over the top of her spectacles to give the three-inch-thick file a long, tired look. "Thanks. I was so hoping you would be able to give that to me today. I don't know what I would have done with all my spare time."

Emma crossed her arms and returned Karen's glare. "Don't give me that, they're due the same time of the month, every month. Along with certain other things, apparently."

Karen wrinkled her nose so that her glasses slid off the bridge of her nose and dangled from their chain across her chest. She buried her face in her hands and started talking into her desk blotter. "Sorry, been a hell of a week."

"If you even start sounding the slightest bit sarcastic again, I'll give you a slap."

"Thanks for your support."

"Mmmmmm . . ." Emma turned to head back to her office, but stopped, and tilted her head. "You look exhausted. Did you get any sleep?"

Karen lifted her nose up from its bed of sticky notes and peered dazedly back at Emma. "I'd like to believe that it was all just a bad dream."

Emma nodded slightly and walked off, leaving Karen to stare at the pile of work at her desk.

So, when do I get to wake up?

Chapter 17

Lunch: thermos, apple, chocolates, and—surprise—a left-over turkey sandwich.

Karen took each article out of her bag and placed them, one by one, on the staff lunch table. She stared for a long time at the turkey sandwich. Finally, she grabbed her thermos, popped the top and hugged the open bottle to her chest, savoring the wafting aroma of coffee, a wonderful glorious French Roast blend with heaps of sugar and lashings of specialty cream.

"Turkey again?" Mavis said as she sat beside her.

Karen could only moan in pleasure as her nostrils were filled with the exotic, caffeine-soaked smell.

Mavis pulled out a shopping bag and withdrew a large bundle from which she started peeling back layers of wax paper. "Peter and I went to that new Asian place last night and got some of these new thingies, but we ordered one too many," said Mavis as her thick fingers revealed numerous diced vegetables ensconced in what looked like a baguette. "It's called a banh mi." Mavis pronounced the word as if it were the sacred name of a bizarrely beautiful and cursed Egyptian jewel.

Karen stared at the soft bread loaded with numerous trappings that peeked out from beneath layers of chili sauce and pork. And then at her turkey sandwich. With real cranberry dressing. And then stared at the banh mi.

"Here," Mavis placed half of the sandwich on Karen's plate.

Karen's mouth hung open.

"Birthday present," said Mavis before adding lamely, "I didn't get you anything else . . ."

"If I could have made a list of presents this morning," Karen hefted the bundle aloft, "this would have been at the top. Short of a large butcher knife . . . Thank you Mavis, you're very kind."

"Well, I can't eat a whole one myself. Lord knows I tried last night."

"We're going to have to work on something called 'gift-giving tact' in the future." Karen giggled around a mouthful of pork. "By

90

the way, I talked to Emma about the dance tonight and she said she'll take care of money and tickets and things."

"Don't worry about lighting, I've got some lovely old lanterns of Gran's that would be perfect."

Karen mentally ticked items off her list. "That just leaves the drinks, but I can handle that." She paused. "You know, I don't know why, but I think I preferred it when we were at each other's throats."

Mavis glanced up at her. "Does seem unnatural, somehow, doesn't it? Shall I pencil you in for Monday for a row if that'll help?"

Karen passed over a piece of chocolate. "God is in his heaven . . ."

"If all my problems could be solved by chocolate, I'd be a diabetic by now," Mavis said, popping the confectionary into her mouth.

Karen stared at her own piece, wondering what else the week could possibly throw at her.

Chapter 18

Friday evening
Little Ivory Public Library

It had been a trying afternoon. Patrick had shown up, but some teacher had got him reading Dickens of all things and had started repeatedly addressing her as "Duchess" until she had banished him to shelf read in the stacks.

Karen found that if she looked intensely busy, patrons would avoid her and check out their own books at the automated kiosk. She had a big night planned, and the last thing she wanted was a customer distracting her. Organizing the dance had seemed like a chance to give Mammoth Man a dinner and show, but she had forgotten that she was the one running the damned thing. Fortunately, Mavis had been nipping in and out of the basement all afternoon setting up the lighting and the band had dropped by to get a key to let themselves in. All Karen had to do was go home, change, get prettied up and pick up the booze.

~ φ ~

Katherine dabbed lightly at the wound with a damp cloth. Enrique winced.

"A small price to pay for rescuing one so beautiful as you." His heavy accent only served to stir her desire for him. She returned the cloth to the basin and finished bandaging his wound. Together, they had made their way to the caves, but Logan had beaten them to it. Instead, they had been met by an ambush and were lucky to escape with their lives. They had found shelter in this small inn and Katherine, although grateful to be alive, was overwhelmed by despair at never being able to save her father who remained trapped in the cave. She gently stroked Enrique's arm, lost in distraction.

Enrique's flesh was smooth and muscled. His hand held hers, and the touch sent electric waves through to the deepest well of her soul. She ached for him. His hand touched her chin and he locked eyes with hers; there she saw her desire matched. In his eyes, she saw her painful longing echoed in his dark pupils. He pulled her closer until their lips were a mere breath apart. Their flesh had never seemed so alive as when they touched for their first kiss.

92

As their tongues met and they became one, their desire mounted and their caresses grew stronger, bolder. His tongue explored hers with expert desire and a burning passion melted her soul. Her fingers unbuttoned his shirt and gently cupped his firm muscles. He leaned back onto the bed, pulling her with him, never letting their lips part or their desire fade. Indeed, their passions flared brighter and fierce—

~ φ ~

The squeaking of the book cart brought her back to the present. Patrick's thin arms steered the metal trolley into position behind the desk and then he foraged in the drawer beneath the register for his paycheck.

Which gave Karen an idea. Before he could leave, she slid the book into her purse, smoothed her hair, and walked over to him. "I need to ask you a favor."

Patrick stood in the main door of the library, his bag slung over one shoulder. "Mrs. W?"

Karen slipped the cover over the typewriter. "I need a bartender for tonight, and it's too late to find anyone else to do it, so what do you say?"

"Err . . . sure," replied Patrick.

Karen pulled on her coat, trying to remember the legal age for serving drinks. "You are eighteen, aren't you?"

"Um . . ." Patrick stuttered doubtfully.

"I said," Karen repeated carefully, "you are eighteen, aren't you, Patrick."

Patrick finally caught on. "Yes, Mrs. W."

"Perfect, just show up at seven-thirty tonight and help set up, okay?"

"No problem."

"Right, I'm off," said Karen as she bustled around the counter, beating him out the door. "See you later."

Karen had one foot out the main doors. Twelve inches more and out. Free.

And then she heard Mavis calling her name.

"Karen, I'm so glad I caught you! This is my brother Luke Iaeste."

Karen turned and found herself facing a rather slight, elderly gentleman with a mop of silver white hair, draped in slacks and a silk shirt.

"Luke, this is my employee, Karen Whittington."

Karen hurriedly reached out a hand and gave a slight shake, awkwardly shifting her purse. "Nice to meet you."

"Luke's coming to the dance tonight," said Mavis sweetly.

Oh my God. She's trying to set me up. Well, thanks all the same but I've got a date to keep and only two hours to prepare for it. "Really," said Karen in her nicest voice. "That's very wonderful, I'm sure."

"Luke's been living in the old country," Mavis said proudly.

"Oh, really," said Karen feigning interest. "Albany?"

"Macedonia," corrected Luke.

"Macedonia," pondered Karen for a moment. "That's northern Greece, isn't it?"

The man's nostrils flared in anger. Karen had never seen anyone do that before. It was kind of impressive.

"No, it is certainly not part of Greece," he growled.

She took in his plaid bow tie and remembered him as the man from the supermarket deli. Her brief, almost-flirtation. Mentally thrown, the best she could manage was: "Really?" Karen desperately groping to recall all those nights she spent helping Tommy and Jimmy with their geography homework. "I was sure that it was."

"It is not, nor has it ever been, part of Greece," Luke's deep baritone voice boomed menacingly. "I know your people have difficulty with geography—"

"I took a whole year of geography," Karen snapped.

"Then I must only suppose that you failed the class."

"I got an A, actually, not that it is any of your business," Karen spat. She turned on Mavis who was hovering anxiously near the counter wringing her hands throughout this exchange. "Sorry Mave, got a lot to do, I'll see you tonight." She turned back to His Macedonian Majesty and gave him a nod before storming out through the door.

She wasn't certain, but she could feel *her* nostrils flaring.

~ φ ~

Karen felt the pressure of hate-filled eyes burrowing into her shoulder blades. She toyed with the sleeve of a white blouse, before delving deeper into the closet to rummage for her favorite pair of flats. Perfect for dancing, those flats. She spied them poking out from beneath some bobbles of yarn that were strewn among shoeboxes and Spiderman-action figures. With a triumphant yell, she tossed them over her shoulder into her bedroom.

She heard a muffled cry from the room beyond waft into the closet.

"Oh relax, Hobbes. I told you I'd let you out before I left."

Mr. Hobbes' ears twitched backwards in anger as he strutted about in his prison. He sniffed at the little bowl of food disdainfully, his thrashing tail constantly bumping against the glass walls. He rotated his upturned nose to glare menacingly at Karen's rear as she crouched at the base of the closet. He probed at the wire-mess that covered the old forty-gallon fish tank, but he only succeeded in catching a claw, which refused to retract. His paw hung, half- suspended, and let out a pitiful meow.

"Oh, for pity's sake." Karen heaved her way out of the wardrobe and struggled to her feet. She crossed to Jimmy's old fish tank to rescue her fave feline. She carefully lifted the cover she had placed on the tank and pried loose his claw.

"There, now be careful," she warned as she gave him a quick loving hug. "I know the ASPCA would hardly approve, but you've ruined me for one date this week and I certainly don't want this one to start off like that." She placed him back inside and withdrew a light camel brown skirt and matching jacket from the closet. She held her Kathleen Turner outfit in front of her and perused her reflection in the figure-length mirror. "And this is one outfit I do not want cat hair on."

Mr. Hobbes let out another indignant wail.

"Oh, wait one second." Karen tossed the outfit on the bed and hurried off to the kitchen, to return moments later with a plate full of leftover turkey scraps. She placed the food within the tank and watched him gobble the fowl; his ears were still firmly pressed against his head though.

Apparently, food would not heal this wound so easily.

"Well, that's dinner for you taken care of and don't worry, I'll let you out before I go." She pulled on the blouse and skirt. She smoothed the fabric of her knee-length skirt down with the palms of both hands and stood once more before the mirror. "Now, considering how my last date went, I wonder what this one will be like?"

She pulled on some stockings and, just for fun, used an eyebrow pencil to draw an old-fashioned seam up the back of each leg. She straightened and primped before her mirror, spying the family portrait sticking out of the jewelry box as she did so. She snatched it up and slipped the photo into her purse.

I need a little luck.

She slid off her engagement ring and held it up, the metal gleaming in the faint light of her bedside lamp. She casually tossed the band aside, landing with a muffled thump on the plush carpet.

She found one of grand-dad's fedoras in a box by some Lego's and popped it on her head, tipped to a jaunty angle and smiled at Mr. Hobbes who lay curled up in a corner of the tank.

"I think it's about time something good happened this week, don't you?"

~ φ ~

Karen toyed with her glass of water, took a sip, swirled the glass around a bit, set it lightly down on the table and picked it up again. Her left knee bounced up and down in a desperate effort to expend all the pent-up energy racing through her. She accidentally bumped against the table leg twice before pressing both feet firmly against the polished oak floorboards.

She propped her elbows up on the table and folded her hands, lacing her fingers together, desperately hoping that someone in the restaurant would comment on her now quite-ringless ring finger.

People miraculously failed to gawp and gape at the fleshy white band of skin on her finger.

Karen stole a glance at her watch in a way that was carefully calculated to appear casual and not to suggest that she was in the slightest bit panicked that her first date in years was eight minutes and thirty-two seconds late. Her eyes flitted desperately around the restaurant to find something to distract her.

"Hello, my name is Karen Whittington," she mentally introduced herself to the old couple sitting at the table by the window. "And I am having my first date in five years," she confided as an aside to the birthday group at the table across from her, "after having slept with my dead ex-husband last night and so betraying my sister to whom he is now married—I would not be feeling too horrible about stiffing that traitorous harpy," she silently explained to the waitress filling her water glass, "if the sex had been any good, which it wasn't really and it has really been irritating me, cause we didn't actually get that far, just sort of passed out next to each other after the hike back . . . some serious spooning though . . . I think?"

Her silent speech trailed off as she realized that forming a support group would mean finding other people who had shared similar experiences. Which would be rather doubtful, all things considered.

She glanced at her watch again (nine minutes, twelve seconds) when Eric strolled in, swathed in a tweed jacket with leather elbow pads and some ridiculously baggy trousers.

She felt a large, joyous smile leap across her face.

With an effort, she managed to keep it plastered to her face as she stared at the bimbo clinging to his arm, dressed in a hideous strapless red dress and pumps, exposing enough skin to have her arrested in Karen's day.

The girl from the library the other night who left before Eric showed up.

The student he was probably meeting for lunch in the deli when she met him on Monday.

They came up to her table.

'In-depth research' my ass.

"Why, hello," Karen greeted them brightly, as a small section of her cerebrum usually reserved for regulating her spleen desperately seized control of her larynx while the rest of her brain went off for a little lie down somewhere.

"Karen!" Eric beamed a friendly smile, his fabulous brown eyes gleaming from beneath the furry mass of his bangs. "You look lovely," he said as he pulled out a chair for his . . . young friend?

Please say friend. Karen's mind perked up and made a quick foray head wise long enough to raise an eyebrow.

Or, mayhap, even say, daughter?

"This is my fiancée, Helen," Eric gestured for the twenty-something wench to sit down. "Darling, this is Mrs. Whittington."

Karen's mind beat a hasty retreat.

She realized she must have blacked out momentarily, because the next thing she knew, she was holding Helen's hand and shaking it slightly, as she might hold a piece of cold spaghetti found clinging to the wall of her sink.

"It's so nice of you to show us around the town and invite us to a party!" Helen gushed. "Eric says you're a librarian!"

She actually sounds excited about it.

"It must be really interesting to have all that knowledge at your fingertips every day." Helen daintily unfolded a napkin and placed it in her lap. "I love going to libraries to do research for my projects, but there really is so little written on Quaternary Paleontology that's really relevant these days, except for some old indexes on fossils from the early 1900s."

Karen could only stare at Helen's perfectly formed painted lips and Helen's gorgeous brown-blond hair that framed Helen's damned sculpted cheekbones and doe-like eyes.

"Helen's receiving her Ph.D. from the university next month," continued Eric as he pounced on the menu, squinting at the tiny print before fumbling in a pocket and withdrawing a pair of spectacles.

"I'm the youngest ever in our program," Helen confided in an excited whisper. "They've never had anyone finish the doctoral program who was under twenty-five before!"

~ φ ~

"No, no, no, Kay." Joe pushed her hands away from the scope. "You twist this to focus." He gestured with thin hands that were already a numbed white from the crisp November air. "If you turn it this way," he swiveled the telescope on its mounting until it was pointing nearly vertical into the night sky, "you can see . . ." He twisted and tweaked some knobs and lenses before stepping back with a flourish. He yanked her up by the waist and dangled her in front of the eyepiece. "This!"

Little Karen looked through the piece of tubing, not knowing about mirrors or reflection or refraction or those other long words that Joe kept on talking about, and she saw, white and gray, the surface of the moon, gleaming back at her. Her older brother had shown her a world outside of Little Ivory.

~ φ ~

Joe was magic. The kind of wonderful, exciting person you rarely get to meet as a kid. They were so amazing because they enjoyed being a kid all over again.

Forty-four years later, Karen let out a long, slow breath and wrapped her arms about her. She stared off into that same night sky which had once seemed so exciting and new. Magical.

Joe was still magic to her. Because he died of course. Only the good . . .

As you grow up, you discover all the faults and flaws that your parents, relatives, and friends all have. It's the ones that you have yourself but almost never see, Karen reflected. Or never want to . . .

But in her mind Joe had no faults, no flaws. She had never known him as anything other than a man who showed her another universe before he went off to War and was killed. But every time she took a long look at the sky and saw the wispy curtain of the Milky Way, she would find herself smiling at the memory of her older brother Joe.

Even now, as she stood in the parking lot of the restaurant leaning against the hood of her car, she discovered that, despite everything, she felt a smile tug at her lips. She was so lost in the stars and her memories that she didn't hear Eric come up from behind her.

"I'm sorry Karen," he said quietly as he came to stand beside her. "I can be a bit thick sometimes, but I remember your moods. I take it by the way you rushed outta there without a word that you were upset, and I think I can figure out why . . . I didn't mean to mislead you in any way," said Eric softly. "I just want to catch up with an old friend and see the town again. You dumped me, remember? It's been so long, it didn't occur to me and you were still wearing your ring . . . I didn't think."

Karen found herself laughing. She could feel all sorts of emotions frothing about inside of her but remarkably, she found herself giggling. "Oh, God."

"Sorry?"

"Oh . . . It's not your fault. Although, yes, that was what I thought, and I am horribly embarrassed."

"Karen—"

"No. No really, I'm fine, but I think I need to be by myself for a bit. You go in there with your . . ." she found she couldn't actually say the word.

"Fiancée," prompted Eric.

"With . . . Helen . . . and have a good time. I have some things to get ready for the party tonight anyway."

"Sure?"

"It's the one thing this week I am sure of. I'll be fine." She gave his arm a tiny squeeze. She turned away and opened her car door and saw him standing there with the night sky soaring above his head. In that moment she realized that she had seen just a little bit of her Joe in Eric. Like Joe, he shared the same boundless energy and childlike enthusiasm.

Eric gave a little wave and walked back into the restaurant.

Unlike Joe, Eric had grown old. But he was still young. Inside.

As Karen fumbled to slot her key in the ignition, she felt something inside her heart quietly burst, and felt the tears drip down her cheeks.

And as she thunked her head against the steering wheel and started clenching and unclenching her fists, she realized that she was not fine.

Not at all.

~ φ ~

Karen stood in the cemetery in front of a block of granite, her shoes wet from the grass.

"Hi Joe. It's me, Kay. I know you can't hear me, or maybe you can. I don't know. I don't know anything anymore. I know it's been a long time since I came to visit. I'm sorry that I've forgotten you for so long. I do miss you. Still.

"I'm a fool Joe. I haven't grown up. I'm fifty and I still haven't grown up. That mess I called a marriage with Michael? Well, I've done it again. Totally misread the situation and got my hopes up, just to have them be dashed all over again. Even after everything that's happened, I was blind. Stupid.

"And tonight, I made a fool of myself again. In front of two probably very nice people. And now I have to go and try and be happy for all these people I invited to this silly thing. Smile, talk, and dance although I'd rather sit here and be with you all night."

She leaned her head gently against the cool, polished rock. She had the nagging feeling that she was forgetting something.

"I don't know why I am always so upset about it. I cried for months after mom got that letter from the Army. I mean, after all you were the one who got shot, not me. I didn't have to lie in the mud and bleed to death. Comparatively, I don't really have any problems, do I? Not really. I suppose at least I'm still alive to complain about it.

"I have to go now, to a party, my birthday party. Sort of. My fiftieth. Never thought I would make it, Joe. Never dreamt I would make it this far. Not sure I ever wanted to." She felt a chill brush against her neck as she sat in the churchyard under the silver glow of a pale moon.

"I better go, the party starts in twenty minutes." She ran a trembling finger along the lines of Joe's name engraved in the stone. "I really wish you were still here." She slowly pulled herself off her knees and started walking out of the graveyard, heading for the glowing yellow lights of the library. "Besides," she added over her shoulder, "if you were still here, I'd have no end of fun; after all, you'd be over *sixty*. I mean, that's wheelchair time!" She chuckled slightly, before pausing. "I need a drink . . ." And then it hit her.

What she had forgotten to do.

"Oh crap. The booze!!"

Chapter 19

Karen snuck in through the back door and stood agape.

The basement had been transformed. The hag—err . . . Mavis, Karen corrected herself, had hung dozens of paper lanterns that fluttered and glowed. Glittering tinsel and silver Christmas garland adorned the serving table while, softly backlit by blue and white lights, the quartet played a soulful wispy number. The Kanes and the Jones rocked about on the dance floor, slowly turning and swaying with the gentle beat.

Karen pushed her shopping cart down the handicap ramp and wheeled it to a halt by the serving table. Bottles clanked and sloshed in protest. Patrick hurriedly helped unload the contents, storing them underneath the linen tablecloth.

"Was wondering when you would come, Mrs. W." Patrick hefted a box of champagne from beneath the cart. "The Cartmans have been asking for punch for the last twenty minutes . . . I was worried what would happen when the bus from the Home got here. You know what they're like."

"Patrick," Karen said breathlessly as she shoved two tequila bottles into a box of Louis L'Amours.

"Yeah?"

"Do me a favor, would you?" Karen paused to uncork a bottle with her teeth.

"Whatever you say."

"Just call me Karen from now on, okay?"

Patrick watched her take a long swig from the bottle. A smile twitched at his lips. "You're the boss."

Karen gave him a little toast with her bottle. "You better start pouring some of that JD into the punch before someone accidentally winds up drinking juice."

"Can't have that!" Patrick cheerfully upended the requested bottle with a flourish.

"I'm just going to stagger over here for a while, okay? Just holler if you need something," Karen managed to burble over her shoulder as she swayed across the dance floor to where Emma was selling tickets.

"Good evening." Emma turned from the front door. "We were wondering if you were going to show up."

Karen peered cautiously into the money drawer. "How is the take so far?"

"About thirty people bought tickets ahead of time." Emma checked her clipboard. "But most are just paying as they come. Hopefully. Oh . . ."

Karen turned to look out into the night to see a hoard of seniors walking up the pavement. "Looks like the whole Home came."

"Elsa said even the chair-bound are coming, just to have a look. You've got the town hopping, Karen!"

Karen watched the throng approach and decided to make a hasty retreat. "I'll get out of the way and let you empty their wallets."

"How much did you spend on alcohol?"

Karen looked quickly at Patrick who was already quaffing down another glass of punch. "Haven't the foggiest. I'll let you know when I get my credit card bill." She watched Patrick reload his cup. "Bills," she corrected.

"Here they come," said Emma as the first of the canes thrashed across the threshold.

"I'm off then."

"Oh, Karen!" Emma fished out a small package from her bag. "Got this for you."

"Ummm . . . Thanks?" Karen stammered, caught off guard.

"It's your birthday present," explained Emma before she was swallowed by geriatrics.

Karen moved back across the floor and opened the package. She peeled back the colored paper to reveal a little silver cross, threaded on a simple chain. She lunged through the mass of people and gave Emma a quick, tight hug. "Thank you," she whispered. "It's the best thing that has happened to me this whole week."

Emma flashed her a quick smile before attending to selling tickets.

Karen turned as she felt a hand on her arm.

"Karen!"

"Claire! Mark!" Karen greeted her friends a little too loudly.

"Have you been drinking?" asked Claire.

"I don't know what you're talking about!" Karen shouted. She looked about anxiously. "You haven't seen a bottle of tequila around, have you? I seem to have misplaced mine."

Claire tactfully ignored her friend's comments and took in her outfit instead. "Pretty snazzy, very forties."

"Knew if I kept it long enough, I'd find a use for it again." Karen eyed the door nervously. "Sheriff Tucker isn't coming tonight, is he?"

"Don't know," said Claire. "Probably, why?"

Karen watched Patrick attempt to fill punch glasses with a not-so-steady hand. "I think, among other crimes I may have committed against friends, relatives, and pets, that I've corrupted a minor."

"I wouldn't worry about it, bound to happen eventually," Mark reassured her. "Besides, I bet Tucker'll be a little corrupted tonight himself."

"One can only hope," muttered Karen.

"What happened to your date?" Mark asked.

Karen suddenly didn't know where to look. After a bewildering moment, she fixed her eyes firmly on Mark's rather wild paisley tie.

Karen saw Claire trod forcefully on his foot. Mark scowled at her for a bit before catching on.

"Care to dance?" Mark offered Karen an outstretched hand.

Karen was a little taken aback. "I guess so," she looked questioningly at Claire. "Is that all right with you?"

"I'm not sure I want you to bring him back!" Claire said good-naturedly. She started walking toward Patrick. "I'll go check on Little Ivory's newest alcoholic."

Karen cautiously took Mark's hand and let herself be led onto the dance floor. At first, they just rocked slowly back and forth together, getting used to each other's movements.

"So," Mark began. "What happened?"

"I did it again. I just walked right in and completely misread the situation. Just saw what I wanted to see."

"Selective vision?"

"Something like that. If I wasn't planning on drinking so much alcohol tonight, I'd probably start to feel very depressed."

Mark surprised her by throwing her outward into a little spin, before pulling her firmly back into his arms once more. "It sounds like you don't pay enough attention to what goes on around you. Too self-absorbed."

"I have no idea what you are talking about."

"Of course not."

The beat of the waltz became faster. Karen found herself struggling to keep up with Mark's footwork.

Mark paused for a moment, considering. "Do me a favor?"

"What?" Karen stumbled onto his toe.

Mark showed no outward discomfort. "Close your eyes."

"That doesn't sound like the best of ideas right now . . . Why?"

"Think of it as a perception test." He carefully steered her to the edge of the dance floor so that they wouldn't careen into any of the other dancers.

"Will it hurt?" she asked, closing her eyes.

"What is pain?"

Karen squinted suspiciously at him through half-closed lids. "The Mark I know burps, has a terrible sense of humor, and is not capable of performing a Lindy." She started breathing heavier for, even as she said it, they started doing just that. Her co-ordination was not at its best right now. "And he certainly doesn't spout philosophical questions."

"Elsa's pâté, I think, has this effect on me. Now this won't hurt, so close your eyes."

"Okay, eyes closed, but don't yell if I step on your toes. Again."

"No worries, my shoes have steel toes. Now, what color is Mavis' hair?"

"What?"

"You heard me. What color is Mavis' hair?"

Karen wrinkled her eyebrows as she tried to pull up a mental flashcard of her friend's face while still concentrating on the beat and her feet. "Brown."

"Brown?"

"No . . . Red. Red-brown."

"I think the word you are looking for is auburn, but close enough. Now, what's Claire wearing?"

Karen tried for a minute to remember what Claire looked like, but her mind was just too fuzzy right now. She opened her eyes. "I don't know—but this doesn't prove anything, I am too far gone right now to play memory *and* stay upright at the same time."

"Okay," conceded Mark. "Let's try a different angle. Jim Montgomery."

"The electrician?"

"Yep, how long have you known him?"

"Well, he's been reading my meter for the past twenty years."

"So, is the following statement true or false: his wife left him to run off with a priest because he gave up photography to find a steady job as an electrician?"

"I have absolutely no idea," replied Karen honestly, although she rather doubted that the plump little man with the funny walk who came to her house every fourth Monday could be an Ansel Adams.

"It's true, actually. Okay, let's try Elsa: has she been writing editorials for the fashion magazines for fifteen years under the name of Fitzroy Bartok?"

"Absolutely false," answered Karen instantly.

"Quite correct. She's been using the name of Kathleen Horner."

Karen boggled a bit at that. She straightened her grip on his shoulders as the pace of the music beat faster and faster. She felt her blood racing, chasing the alcohol out of her system, could feel the sweat on her brow. She was surprised to find that she was actually enjoying this. "All this proves is that I'm not up on my gossip. It has nothing to do with my relationship with men."

"Claire," Mark said, firmly twisting Karen around and dipping her slightly so that she was facing her old friend. "True or false?"

Uh oh. Karen didn't like the sound of where this was headed.

"Claire is three months pregnant."

Karen stared at the upside-down image of her friend, dressed in quite a nice floral purple and gold number which hung off her shoulders and showed off her breasts, before sweeping down to her ankles, just barely noticeable, was a soft swollen bulge at her waist.

106

Oh.

"Well?" asked Mark, pulling her upright as the number ended and the band put down their instruments.

But she's forty-two! "Why didn't she say anything?"

"Karen, not everyone tells everybody the story of their life in the first five minutes of meeting them."

"But I've known her for years! Why didn't she say anything?" Karen almost lost her footing completely; only Mark's arm held her upright.

"After all those years, she shouldn't have to." Mark pressed his point home.

"You mean, if I just bothered for one moment to—"

"To look, yeah."

"I need another drink," said Karen as they walked back to Claire. "I thought you said this wouldn't hurt."

"I said probably. Besides, it's false."

Karen stood stock-still and flashed him a dangerous look. "You mean—"

Mark shook his head. "And thank God for that, we have three already. But you still *thought* she was. Point taken?"

Karen gave Mark a queer look. "Remind me to steer you clear of any pâté in the future."

~ φ ~

Karen had returned Mark to his proper owner and fawned over her newly not-pregnant friend in her wonderful new dress. Now, however, Karen sat in one of the chairs lining the edge of the dance floor and watched the mature population of Little Ivory have a little fun.

Karen had specifically instructed Patrick not to put out folding chairs, but apparently, he hadn't listened to her once again. Chairs around a dance floor encouraged wall-flower-type people to sit in the stupid things. Encouraging them, giving them a place to be instead of out having fun. Why did people like those come to dances like this if they know all they are going to do is sit and watch other people have fun? What were they thinking?

"What are you thinking?" asked Claire as she sat down next to her friend.

"Nothing," said Karen a little too quickly.

"Do you wanna talk about it?"

"No. Maybe tomorrow. Not tonight. Not tonight."

"Oh."

They sat like that for a while and stared at the melee of dancers who spun, swayed, and sloshed about the dance floor.

"Where did Mark learn how to dance?" Karen asked, eventually.

Claire gave a little laugh. "From me. For our wedding. He didn't want to look like a klutz in front of two hundred people. We spent every weekend for two months beforehand practicing."

"He is good." Karen admitted.

"Tell me about it. Do you have any idea how surprised I was? I knew him for four years before we got married and I never saw him dance once before. Mind you, I think he was more surprised to find out that he actually liked doing it."

Karen looked up to see Patrick waltzing across the dance floor with Jessica, the bank teller.

"I'm almost too afraid to ask," Karen said quietly. "But who's working the bar?"

Claire half-stood up to see over the top of her friend's head before plopping back into her chair. "That would be Sheriff Tucker."

"Well, that's definitely one big worry out of my life," said Karen flatly.

Claire smoothed out her dress, not designed for metal folding chairs. "Judging by your tone, I take it then that your guardian angel has not been doing his job lately."

"Right now, I need a fleet of 'em piloting a squadron of stealth bombers. Or just a miracle. I'm not fussy right now."

"I'm glad you haven't lost your sense of humor."

"No, but I am getting moody. Must be sobering up . . ." Karen trailed off, tilting her empty cup at Claire.

"I can take a hint." Claire snatched up the glass. "Double?"

"Yes, please."

Claire rose and started weaving her way through the dancers, sidestepping the odd walker as she made her way toward Sheriff Tucker.

Karen watched the world spin around her. Watched Patrick stumble and trip as he tried to follow Jessica in a simple Charleston. Silly girl, wrong era completely. Not that it mattered really; no one was paying the slightest attention to the two youngsters. Karen wondered how Jessica had gotten in, but looking round the room, noticed that Emma wasn't so much Seniors Only orientated as Cash Orientated.

The dance floor had filled up during the first few songs. Karen looked at her watch to discover that it was only nine-thirty, yet there was barely room to stand. Everyone had drinks in one hand, the other filled with canes, walkers, or clutching each other's hands. The Hendricksons, the family hardware owners, were gently holding each other in their arms, staring into each other's eyes, oblivious to the others around them. Mavis was dancing with some tall bald thing, wherever she dragged him from, but she was still smiling. And the Martins, her neighbors of twenty years, were laughing at each other's attempts to swing dance.

Even Elsa was dancing, and judging by his lumpish form and khaki slacks, she was sashaying with Mavis's brother of all people. Good luck to her. People she hadn't seen in years were gently swaying back and forth or sipping punch with a wonderful gleam in their eyes. The dance floor was filled with glaring white, blue, gray, and brown-hued mops of hair that bounced in the flickering candle lights.

"It's amazing," Karen told Claire when she returned with the beverages.

"All out of tequila but thought you'd manage to survive on champagne." Claire handed her a flute. "What's amazing?"

"This." Karen waved her hand at all the people crammed into the basement.

Claire looked around the room and nodded. "People are having a great time in a way I don't think they have in years. And you did it, Karen."

"What?" Karen was only half-listening as she watched a couple of old guys dancing with each other in jest to the mild amusement of a pair of old ladies standing by the band. She was sure one of the prats was her old math teacher, Mr. Gannon. Karen giggled as he dipped the other man and feigned to drop him.

And then it sunk in. They were all here, all this was here, because of her. Because she had decided to do something and went through with it. She felt pride surge through her, something she hadn't felt since she passed her first job interview. She could do it. She *had* done it.

Karen's cheeks flushed as a rush of adrenaline flowed through her. She could do anything. She mentally reviewed everything that had happened this whole day, this whole stupid, damned embarrassing, stupidly ridiculous, insane week . . . and she laughed.

She turned to her old friend and wanted to blurt out what she was feeling, what had happened at dinner, what a great friend she was, but she didn't. Instead, Karen smiled her biggest smile and raised her champagne glass in a toast. As her mind swelled with all the thoughts and images racing through her head and how to express them, all she could say was: "To the next chapter!"

Claire gamely raised both her glass and her eyebrow at her friend's sudden change of mood. "To new adventures."

They clinked glasses.

As Karen sipped her champagne, she glanced back across the dance floor, her gaze attracted to Elsa's forest-green dress, and her eyes brushed with those of Mavis' brother. Elsa had evidently said something funny, for he was in mid-laugh, his emerald-green eyes flashing in the light.

What color is Mavis' hair?

Claire must have noticed that Karen held her glass to her mouth, not drinking. Frozen. "Karen?"

But Karen wasn't listening. She could only stare at his eyes, crinkled around the edges, the skin of his chin loose and wobbling with his laughter. Her mind mentally tugged at that loose flesh, pulling it tighter, while softly erasing the crow's feet around his eyes, letting adolescent freckles skitter across his cheeks, letting color wash across his scalp like a splash of wine—

Brown—no, red, red brown.

Oh no.

—the waves swallowed the Taco Palace beneath her, sucking his hand out of her grasp and she watched his eyes, those emerald-green eyes, slip under the waves—

. . . And suddenly his flesh sagged again, his hair shot through with white, the freckles smoothed to cream. But she was still looking into the same eyes.

110

"I don't believe it," Karen gasped, lowering her glass. She turned to Claire. "Why him? Of all people? Tell me this isn't happening?"

Claire looked at her oddly, but before she could say anything, Karen was on her feet.

If it was him.

If.

If, if, if . . .

Karen had had enough If's.

And suddenly, she was walking toward him—Luke—walking toward Luke and doing something about an impossible dream because she simply couldn't just sit there and wonder, let him go by accident. She was doing it, doing something about it. But she didn't have a clue what she would do when she got there.

Karen had almost reached him when she felt a hand on her arm. She spun around, snatching her arm away.

"You?" sputtered Karen. "What are you doing here? I thought you left!"

"Karen," Michael said, placing a hand on her shoulder. "I still haven't told you why I'm here."

Karen shook off his hand and took a long sip of her champagne as she turned back to her prey.

But he was gone.

So was Elsa.

Fudge.

Karen grabbed Jessica as she bobbed past. "Where is he? Where did he go?"

"Who?" Jessica's eyes were wide as she tried to back away.

"Where is Elsa and that man she was with?" Karen demanded, spittle flying.

Jessica dodged the barrage but finally seemed to realize what she was talking about. "Oh them, they left just a sec ago. Together."

Karen wanted to scream. She wanted to kick and hit something, but let Jessica go.

Kicking and hitting were much better directed at someone else. What else were ex-husbands good for?

"And you," she yelled, turning on Michael. "Why did you sleep with me?"

Karen was only peripherally aware that people had stopped dancing to stare at them. At Mrs. Whittington arguing with her dead husband.

She was definitely not looking forward to Sunday service this week.

"I still haven't told you why I'm here," Michael said quietly.

"I told you, I don't care. I am not the slightest bit interested," Karen insisted, her gaze fixed on a wrinkled poster of a Burmese pigmy. And if you don't tell me why the hell you did come here, I'll start screaming for all I'm worth.

"Karen—it's about Beth . . ."

~ φ ~

Karen sat at her desk in her office and forced herself to take deep breaths. Beneath her, she could still hear the quartet and the babble of chatter from the party. She folded her hands in her lap, pressed her knees close together, placed her feet side by side, and stared straight ahead.

Looking at nothing.

Feeling nothing.

Wishing she really felt nothing.

She didn't know how long she sat like that. She didn't care. The room was a sloshy curtain of tears and that was fine.

Karen found herself staring at the window while her hands moved themselves. Her fingertips expertly flipped the catch on her purse and pried the clasp open, knocking over a small plastic vase filled with daisies that clattered upon the tabletop. She barely noticed. Her hands reached inside and took out her slice of history.

The sky was a hazy blue that summer Sunday. Michael had been sprawled on a blanket, an island of terry cloth in the grass moat that was the front lawn. Tommy and Jim were caught in bizarre postures as thin lines of water hung suspended in mid-air from their water pistols. Grandpa was at the front gate with Uncle Leo, arguing with the postman about football or cards or whatever. Leo had a pained frown indicating that he was losing yet again. Karen smiled at the image of herself with long brown hair, dressed in a ghastly eighties outfit, her hands gesturing wildly in the air as she was discussing with Aunt Margaret about where to have the family picnic this year.

Karen gazed at the picture of her happy family and wondered how she could be such a horrible person. She held the three-inch by four-inch sheet of Kodak paper in her hands: her symbol of her happy past. A passport to all those years that had been good. Not good, she corrected herself, wonderful. And all hers. Her wonderful family, all of them. Grandpa and Leo, Tommy and Jim, and even Michael. Her wonderful family.

Her hands started to shake.

In all the years that Karen had stared at her treasured image, she had never once wondered who had *taken* the picture. Who had been holding the camera? Who had given her a past?

All she could hear was Michael's voice echoing over and over again in her head.

"It's about Beth . . . Karen, she wanted me to make things right between you . . . Beth has cancer. She's dying."

Karen ran to the bathroom and threw up.

Chapter 20

Friday bedtime
Little Ivory Public Library

Karen sat on the steps outside of the library, looking up at the sky, her eyes closed. The clouds had swept in again, so she couldn't see the stars, but she felt a cool breeze on her face. She had crept downstairs after everyone had left, having watched the cars and buses leave from her office window. She decided to have a nice little sit down before attempting to drive home. She desperately wanted to go home and cuddle with Mr. Hobbes under her down comforter, but she was still too inebriated to even contemplate driving.

Or even pronounce the word "contemplate" for that matter.

So, she just sat there, her eyes closed, waiting to sober up. Which was why she didn't see him when he tripped over her.

"My apologies." Luke peered down at her.

Karen didn't have enough emotion left to be surprised. She was completely drained. "Oh—it's you." Karen slowly wiped away her tears. "Fancy running into you here. Small town."

"Are you okay?"

"No," she sniffled, "but I will be." She stared at the ground. "I'll be fine." The man of her dreams was wearing quite sharp loafers. "I'm not the one who needs help."

"Do you need a lift somewhere?" He fumbled for his car keys. From her stationary position, Karen could see that he was only managing to remain upright with great difficulty.

No wonder he was so friendly, she thought. He probably doesn't even remember who I am. It would be nice to see you wrap yourself round a tree, but I'm certainly not going to let another incident like Sara's happen again.

She grabbed the keys.

"I am in no condition to drive," she insisted. "And neither are you."

He wobbled above her. "I cannot leave you to sit here by yourself at this time of night."

How heroic. Like I'm the one in trouble. His thick European accent was growing on her, despite the smell of his breath. "I can't let you drive like that."

They stared at each other, each grimly determined, in the logical stubbornness born of intoxication.

Karen found herself with the one person she had spent the whole night—no, her whole life—looking for and now she didn't really want to be around him at all.

The man of her dreams was an argumentative man with bad breath and couldn't hold his liquor.

Typical.

Karen levered herself to her feet. "This is silly. Come on, let's get some coffee."

Luke's head nodded, although his mind still seemed to be considering the offer. The nodding threatened to topple his whole body. Karen placed a hand on his arm to steady him.

He started to hobble forward, leaning on his new human crutch.

Apparently, we're going for coffee, she thought.

His arms were not particularly muscular, but she probably wasn't seeing him at his best. Then another thought struck her: "What happened to Elsa?"

"Who?"

Men. Karen sighed. "You have no idea what I'm talking about do you? Never mind, forget it." I'll find out on Monday soon enough. Although judging from the purple welt on his cheekbone, Elsa was alive and kicking. "By the way, I looked it up."

"Looked what up?"

"Your country—Macedonia was part of Greece—"

"But—"

"—and was also part of Yugoslavia until 1991 when it became what we know as modern Macedonia."

"As I am correct, I do not see—"

"—You should see that you shouldn't get snotty with people until your country is older than my underwear, or my cat for that matter. When I took geography, your country didn't even exist; hell, when my sons took geography, it didn't exist. So, don't be such a snob. But . . ." She took a long breath. "I apologize for putting my foot in my mouth and I do apologize for my ignorance."

They started walking on in silence. The town of Little Ivory was silent and dark at this early hour. Only the row of streetlights glowed in the night.

His silence began to irritate her. Was he really having this effect on her, or was it all in her head?

"You make much money tonight, yes?" ventured Luke as they turned down Main Street.

"Yes," Karen said as she half-remembered a conversation with Emma. "Well, not *much* exactly, but some."

"What are you going to do with it?"

Karen blew out a long breath. "Get rid of a whole load of old books, I suppose. Well, we were going to spend the money mailing the old books and magazines to prisons and ship the children's books and primers to kids in developing countries, but we don't have anything like enough money for that."

He paused, considering. "I think my company would."

"Really?" asked Karen, amazed.

"Yes." He nodded emphatically. "There is much desire in our country—and others to improve English. These would be very useful."

"Thank you." Karen was slightly awed. "You don't have pointy ears under there, do you?"

"It would also be useful for my company: tax write-off!" He laughed mightily at that and Karen found herself staring at those little crows' feet and smiling.

Something puzzled her. "Tell me, why does Mavis have red hair?"

"Our mother was Irish. She and Mavis came to live here. I stayed with my father. Mother was what they call a Ginger, yes? Why?"

"Never mind," muttered Karen as she steered them through the door of Anna Mae's doughnut shop that was open twenty-four hours to supply the late-night student crowd with caffeine and sugar. With an effort, she dumped Luke in a booth before slumping onto the seat opposite. She waved two fingers at Mae, who took the hint and set two steaming cups of coffee in front of them before disappearing in a cloud of menthol-scented smoke.

Karen looked up from her coffee to find the Macedonian studying her face. His bushy eyebrows concertina-ed into a frown. "Have been crying, you?"

She rubbed her swollen eyes and let out a groan. "Who are you, Perry Mason?"

He stared at her, that same puzzled expression on his face.

"Sorry," mumbled Karen. "Does your English get worse when you drink, or does it improve? I can't tell."

He fixed her with a steady gaze. "Do you want to talk about it?"

Do you want to know that my sister was so desperate to make amends with me that she sent her husband to sleep with me so we would be even? Do I want to tell you what an unbelievable mess my life has been? Yes, please yes, please tell me that I am not messed up, I'm not a bad person, yes, I want you to tell me that.

"No, not really," she said instead. "I want to hear about Macedonia."

See Mark, she thought, I do pay attention.

They talked through eight cups of coffee and three packs of donut-holes. They talked about east and west, the plus and minuses of cats and dogs, of planets and family, of boats and books. They talked until the sun came up over the hill and flooded Little Ivory with a golden light that glittered through the shifting green foliage that lined Main Street.

Karen found herself staring at the sludgy mixture of coffee grounds and sugar grains that swirled at the bottom of her coffee cup and realized that she was enjoying herself. She discovered that yes, she was okay, actually. She could handle it, one day at a time.

I'm starting to feel grown up, she realized. Just a little. She smiled to herself. Still a long way to go yet, though.

~ φ ~

Eventually, exhaustion and sobriety brought an end to the night. He walked her back to the parking lot and stood awkwardly by her open car door. Instead of experiencing irritation with his silence, Karen was overwhelmed with anticipation. In her head dwelt the image of Kate and Enrique, panting for release.

Finally, Karen could stand it no more, leaned forward, and kissed him.

~ φ ~

117

As their tongues met and they became one, their desire mounted and their caresses grew stronger, bolder.

~ φ ~

His mouth tasted of stale beer laced with the sticky-sweet residue of coffee and donuts.

~ φ ~

His tongue explored hers with expert desire and a burning passion that melted her soul.

~ φ ~

Karen had leaned in too far, too fast; there was a clink as their teeth bounced against each other; her whole skull echoed with the vibration. She pulled back, putting her hands over her mouth. She started to shake, her eyes watering.

Luke moved closer, concern evident on his face.

Karen shook her head and lowered her hands, her cheeks shiny and wet in the bright summer sun. She took his arms, and still laughing, stepped back into his warm embrace once more.

And when he asked her to join him for dinner that night, she found herself saying: *No, thank you, it has been a long week.*

But what are you doing next Friday?

Chapter 21

Karen answered the doorbell and was greeted by warm, double fudge brownies. With walnuts.

"Do you ever feel like you work for *Meals on Wheels*?" Karen whisked the brownies into the kitchen and returned with two plates and tall glasses of milk.

"You're hardly an invalid." Claire popped a couple of stray walnut pieces into her mouth. "Besides, I think they're supposed to bring healthy food to the doorstep, not food with enough saturated fat that it would make bacon look like a daily vitamin. You've just had a bad week, that's all."

Karen's dining room table was dressed in a fresh cream linen cloth; the curtains were pulled back, and the windows were thrown open, letting the hazy late afternoon sun wash over them. They sat sipping the cold drinks and enjoying the sensation of the condensation glisten on their hands as they stared into the nothingness. The gargantuan willow trees shifted languidly in the slight breeze, gently brushing the heads of the garden gnomes that inhabited the front lawn. The street was empty of any passing cars. The fields beyond were lush and green, silent in their lazy undulations.

Utterly restful and contemplative.

It had been irritating Karen all afternoon.

Sleep deprivation was not helping. Nor was the minor hangover. A short nap had been attempted but provided neither rest nor escape. So many emotions good, bad, marvelous, and fearful churned her stomach. Even Mr. Hobbes had been avoiding her all day.

Karen grasped her napkin tightly. "I want to do something."

"A team diet might be good after we finish these." Claire dabbed at her lips with a napkin. "Are you sure you're ready to do something? No offense, but you look like you could use a few weeks of sleep."

Karen shook her head, watching the tip of Mr. Hobbes' tail flit about between the gnomes. "My body won't let me." She

119

contemplated the remaining dark crumbs on her plate. "I think it's on strike."

"Your body has its own union? That's kind of impressive." Claire picked up the plates and took them into the kitchen. The clatter of dishes brought a scratching on the screen door.

Shortly, Claire returned to her chair. Mr. Hobbes leapt into her lap, purring contentedly. "You know, everyone had a great time last night despite the impromptu floor show. Or perhaps," she reflected, "because of it. Anyway, off topic, but I got to speak to the mayor last night about running for town council next year."

Karen was staring at Mr. Hobbes. Claire was rubbing his belly. He *never* let her do that. Karen felt inadequate. "Are you going to do it?"

"Sounds like fun, in an odd way." All four of Mr. Hobbes' legs were stretched up to the ceiling, and a trickle of drool dangled from his mouth, his purring heavy with ecstasy, his fur burning gold in the orange light of the setting sun.

Traitor.

Karen returned her attention to Claire. "So, full-time job, husband, kids, delivering chocolate to the needy, and now, politician?" Karen's eyebrows were set on 'high.' "Is your new time machine red or blue?"

Claire tickled the furry chin and shrugged, searching for an answer. "What can I say? I have a hard time sitting still . . . Drives me nuts, lying around when there's something needing doing."

Karen opened her hands and let the shredded remains of her napkin fall to the table. She couldn't put it off any longer. She started picking the tiny, white bits of paper off the linen. "Do you mind looking in on my plants this week?"

Claire tilted her head. "Of course. What's up?"

"Something I've been putting off." Karen shook the debris into the wicker waste bin beside the table. "Sort of a 'Do It Yourself Project.'"

Chapter 22

Patrick rolled the empty book cart behind the front desk as the last of the day's patrons departed. He glanced at the multi-colored game of solitaire that Karen was dealing on the counter.

"What on earth are you doing?"

"Circulation," explained Karen, expertly flipping through the index cards. "Computer's busted. EMP or something," she muttered vaguely. "So, it's back to the old-fashioned method. Pain."

Patrick's eyes widened in disbelief. "An electromagnetic pulse effect? I thought those could only be generated by a nuclear explosion."

"Nuclear explosion, multidimensional thingamuwhutzit, combined effects of sixty perimenopausal women in the basement, I don't know, I'm not a computer expert for God's sake!" Karen slapped the final card on the desk and stalked to her station. She slumped down in her seat and started filling the cardboard box that sat atop. Paperclips, files, post-its, pencils, photos, sneakers . . .

She looked over the rim of the box to see Patrick still standing there with a stricken look on his face.

"Sorry, Patrick," Karen stuffed her flats in the box. "That was four gallons of coffee talking. The stupid computer just went down on me, I haven't had any sleep and to be honest it's the last thing I need right now. It's been a bit of a rough week and I still have to cram Mr. Hobbes into a cat-carrier. Thank God it's Saturday."

Patrick leaned on the counter and eyed the rapidly filling box. "Where are you going?

"Hotel near my sister's hospital," Karen said as she stuffed a pair of heels into the box.

"Sorry, I didn't know," mumbled Patrick, idly toying with a pot of fake flowers. "Is it bad?"

"Pretty bad, yes."

"How long will you be gone?"

"I'll be gone . . . I'll be gone as long as it takes." Karen took a step back. "You haven't seen my tennis shoes, have you?"

"Uhh . . . no, don't think so." Patrick's eyes wandered about, eventually alighting on a brass-framed photo sticking out of the top of the box, showing a pair of young men in graduation gowns. "Who're they?"

Karen plucked up the picture and stared at it for a moment. "My sons, Tommy and Jimmy."

Patrick took a closer look at the duo with duplicate mops of curly hair. "I didn't know you had twins."

"Yep," said Karen, plucking her photo back and tossing it into the box. "Genetics. Me, my grandmother, and my mother too . . ." she trailed off as she stared into the distance.

"Umm . . . Mrs. Whittington?"

She gave him a long look.

"Err . . . sorry . . . Karen?"

"Yes, Patrick?"

"Why do you keep eight pairs of shoes at your desk?"

Karen waved a pair of bunny slippers at him. "Patrick, if you learn nothing else from me—"

"Yeah?"

"Never question a woman's footwear."

"Yes, boss."

Chapter 23

Saturday evening
109 Willow Leaf Lane

Katherine held the blade clenched between her teeth, her hands working furiously with the keys. One after another, she jammed each into the lock of Enrique's manacles, but none was the right one.

Cursing the gods around the sliver of steel with mumbled words, she slotted the last key into the lock and gave it a savage twist. The heavy iron cuff clattered to the floor, and Enrique lurched sideways, his weight suspended by the last chain on his remaining wrist. Beside him, similarly manacled, her father groaned in pain.

Katherine was pressed against the moist and gritty stone wall, as Enrique's body slumped against her. She gently levered herself out from under him and reached for the other manacle.

Then she heard a scuff on the flagstones behind her.

She whirled around, her blond hair flailing in the air as she turned to face—

~ φ ~

Hairbrush, Karen remembered. She reached over to her bedside table and grabbed the object and chucked it onto the foot of her bed.

~ φ ~

—to face Logan, who stood at the top of the stairs of the dungeon, his rifle trained on Katherine.

Katherine snatched the knife out of her mouth and held it before her, stepping in front of Enrique, her eyes flashing defiantly as her nemesis calmly descended the stairs. Even in the dim light of the dungeon, Katherine could see his tiger-white teeth as Logan grinned at his prey.

~ φ ~

Toothbrush.

~ φ ~

"I've been waiting for you to come." Logan's curly dark hair was braided tightly behind his head, his skin was pulled taught like

a wraith, his eyes wide and filled with hate. He gestured with his gun at the tortured men who lay half-suspended on the wall. "I didn't know how much longer they would last."

Katherine said nothing. The knife in her hand never wavered.

"Did you really think you would get away?" Logan asked, his tone suggesting that he was honestly curious. "Did you think we would let you escape with the Starfire? We searched for decades for it and you think I'd just let you walk away with it?" Logan moved closer to Katherine. "You were nothing to him." He gestured to Enrique. "One night to satisfy his lust, that is all. He was only after the Starfire," he said simply. "This could never end any other way. You know that, I think."

Part of Katherine's mind was busy calculating angles and distance to the rifle while ticking precious seconds off the timetable established in her head. The other half felt her soul crumble, as if swallowed by her own fears, for deep down, she knew that Logan spoke the truth.

Behind her, Enrique groaned in agony, twisting in his chain as he struggled to regain consciousness.

"And you do this to him? Just to get me back?" Katherine spat.

"They know that the Starfire exists, that it isn't a myth," Logan said. "They have to die."

"But torture?" whispered Katherine.

Logan raised the butt of the rifle to his shoulder, framing Katherine's frail form in the sights. At this range, there was no way that he could miss. "Once you had found the Starfire, this was the only way to make sure that you wouldn't return to England. I knew you wouldn't leave, not without your father."

Katherine tightened her grip on the hilt of the dagger and slowly pulled her arm back. One chance, her mind flashed. Only one chance.

"But now it's mine. Forever," Logan pulled the trigger.

Enrique screamed.

Katherine whipped the knife up and out of her hand as she threw herself to the side, her face burning from the cloud of cordite and power that sprayed outward, as her side was slammed by the—

~ φ ~

124

Hair spray, Karen remembered. She closed the novel and got out of bed once more, careful not to disturb Mr. Hobbes who was snuggled up against her pillow and retrieved the bottle out of the bathroom and tossed it in the suitcase.

And there she saw the black dress that she had subconsciously packed.

For the funeral.

Karen brushed the novel off her bed and curled around Mr. Hobbes, listening to him purr as she stared off into nothingness, feeling his warmth against her side, his life against hers.

She stayed that way for a long time, the book unfinished beside her.

Chapter 24

How old is the world?

How many sounds have you heard?

How big is Little Ivory?

Do you measure with a yardstick, by miles, or with a ruler? Do you measure the surface of each peak, each puddle, boulder, and blade of grass? Take calipers and mark out each cobble, each pebble? Smaller still, do you measure on the micron level each single grain of dirt, the distance each electron orbits around its spinning nucleus?

In short, how long does it take to get somewhere you really don't want to go?

Karen watched the wipers stutter across her windshield, making long, gray streaks that obscured the road ahead, blurring the ruby stoplight like a smear of jelly. A faint drizzle misted across the glass, not quite enough to ease the path of the wiper blades. The moisture of her breath was clouding up the interior, making an already drab day seem even more surreal and dream-like.

When the ruby smear turned a vague greenish color, Karen absently flicked on the defroster and listened to the hum of the fans as they wafted warm air into the car. As she drove on, she noticed a mother on the sidewalk, dragging a little figure behind her bedecked in a yellow duck suit. The child found a huge puddle beneath an elm tree and splashed up and down joyfully, much to the disgust of the soaked parent. Karen turned back to the road as a dark-blue bread van parked by the sidewalk obscured her view of the family, switching off the wipers as they started to groan in protest.

Karen let the water droplets sit on her windshield, watching as they grew larger before flowing together to form mega-drops. Eventually they would wobble before leaping toward the roof, running up the windshield in miniature streams that randomly switched paths as they raced for the top. Then, with a flick of her thumb, she would key the "Intermittent" switch and watch with glee as her canvas was swept clear, and the game began anew.

As she tired of her game, she noticed a brown Buick was drawing alongside in the other lane, edging forward, just ahead of her. As they passed a cluster of post office boxes, she began to take the advances personally. When the bumper of the Buick passed her hood, Karen calmly raised an eyebrow and pressed down firmly on the accelerator. She gave a little mocking wave as she flew past, leaving a blissfully unaware driver to wallow in her wake.

At the next red light, she rather sheepishly fiddled with her radio with intense concentration as the Buick pulled up alongside her.

Karen purposefully started the car again very slowly, letting the puzzled competition get as far away as possible. As she rolled on ahead, she had time to notice the elm tree. Its bark was dark with the sheen of water, and its thick trunk bore boughs of green leaves that glistened wetly in the misty morning. A gentle breeze was shaking large droplets off; they landed with visible *plops* into the puddle beneath.

Must be one of the few survivors from Dutch Elm disease, there's always some no matter what the blight.

As she accelerated, she cast a look in her mirror at the tree that stood proudly in its two-by-two-foot haven of dirt surrounded by a world of concrete pavement.

Suddenly the tree no longer looked as tall and beautiful as it had a moment before.

Karen gave Mr. Hobbes a comforting stroke as she drove on past the bakery. Mr. Hobbes gave a little cat sigh before shoving his face deeper into the blanket. He had given up his pitiful meowing after she had let him out of his carrier box—content now to hide his gaze from the terrifying world that streaked past the windows and no doubt sleep as much as possible in the hopes it would all be gone when he awoke.

Karen pulled her hand away as she realized that she wasn't sure which of them she was trying to comfort. She had a nasty suspicion it wasn't Hobbes . . .

She pulled up to the red light and stared at the elm tree again.

In short, how many times am I going to drive around this block?

With one last flick of the wiper blades, she finally turned into the hospital parking lot.

~ φ ~

Karen listened to the *swish* as the glass doors of the hospital automatically parted to let her into the foyer. Karen paused on the threshold and felt a triumphant smirk crease her lips.

Today, at least, I exist.

Then she looked down at her feet and saw the subtle hump in the carpet that delineated the edges of the weight sensor.

Karen pursed her lips.

She strode into the foyer, passed the many chairs filled with children coughing and the various assortments of casts and bandages that adorned the injured, and headed for the elevators. She watched her feet: one foot then another, step by step . . .

What was it they say? A journey of a thousand miles begins with a single step? Karen mentally held up the cliché and examined it from every angle, dissecting it for deeper meaning.

Distraction behavior, said Elsa's little voice in her head.

Oh, shut up.

Every journey begins with a single step, she repeated to herself. But the first step of a journey is merely the result of the last step of the last journey, right? So, the first step of every journey that you can ever take or have ever taken was in that living room where you took that very first step across the carpet as a baby and fell into your mother's arms. And that step was the result of your parent's first steps and on and on . . .

As she passed the counter, Karen noticed out of the corner of her eye that there was a snack machine in an alcove. It was nestled between two cloisters and a potted plant; *New Zealand pine*, read the tag. Karen found herself feeding the vending machine every nickel that she could dredge up from the depths of her purse.

So, reasoned Karen slowly, every footstep and every journey that every man has ever taken from Genghis Khan to Buddha to the man who cleaned William Shakespeare's chamber pot to Oliver North . . . every step that anyone has ever taken in the history of the entire world has led me, Karen Whittington, to this point, to this choice:

[A5] or [D9].

Choosing between trail mix or chocolate cupcakes.

128

Karen leaned heavily against the keypad and gently closed her eyes.

I don't want to be here.

~ φ ~

Karen heard a quiet *plunk* beside her.

Why is this so hard to do?

Why can't I handle this?

I can deal with Mavis and Michael and Luke and the rest of the loonies in that town and I can sort out my life, but why can't I deal with this?

Why do I still *hate* her?

The quiet little voice in her head answered:

My sister is lying three floors up in a bed with tubes stuck in her. Alone.

Dying.

The sister I haven't had for ten years.

The sister I won't have in another few months.

Why isn't it me up there? We are identical twins . . . why did she get cancer but not me?

Karen reached inside the machine, took out the little cellophane-wrapped package and sat on a hard-plastic chair that lay next to the water fountain. She munched quietly on her trail mix.

I don't have a choice anymore.

The peanuts felt dry and gritty in her mouth.

It's not up to me.

~ φ ~

The elevator doors sprang apart with a tiny *ping* that echoed around the little space.

Karen stepped out into the hall, clutching her little purse to her chest as she sniffed the dry, bitter air of the corridor. She shuffled past numerous green doors with names and warning signs scrawled across them in bright yellow lettering. The large plexiglass window that looked onto the children's ward challenged her, but she couldn't look at the little bald faces that peered back at her. She buried her nose into her coat and hurried on.

On to Room 345.

She stopped, her hand resting on the doorknob.

It struck her that she had no idea what to say to this person.

This person. Her sister. Her sister that she hadn't seen in ten years was a stranger.

What could she say?

'*Hello,*' didn't quite do it.

'*Sorry?*'

'*Sorry for stealing the love of your life and ruining your youth and abandoning you and hating you and all along you were the one who gave everything you had so that I could be happy . . . did you send your husband to seduce me to make up for what you did to me because . . . because you . . .*'

Karen suddenly found herself taking short, heaving breaths.

She turned the knob and entered the room.

And Karen saw her own deathbed.

It had been so long since she had seen . . .

It was her . . . she . . . her . . . they . . . were dying.

Even when you are a twin, sometimes, just for a moment, when you see your other, all you see is yourself.

Elizabeth—Beth was lying between deathly white linen sheets, her nose and mouth obscured by the green plastic of the respirator. What was left of her gray hair was tangled in the elastic straps. Blue and purple veins throbbed along her forehead and neck. Her arm lay across her chest, clear tubes sucking and feeding strange fluids into obscene holes in her skin. Her eyes were closed.

. . . because you loved me that much.

Karen realized that she didn't have to say anything at all; Beth couldn't hear her.

She suddenly discovered that she had so much she wanted to say.

~ φ ~

Karen spent that evening and most of the next by Beth's bedside alone, wringing her hands and staring out the window, watching the cars ebb and flow out of the parking lot below, while busily crocheting with massive bobbles of wool. Mr. Hobbes spent most of that time huddled in a closet at Michael and Beth's town house.

Karen had met Michael at the door, handed him Mr. Hobbes' travel box and walked away. She had spent last night in a Holiday Inn.

There were times to deal with things and times not to.

130

Too much to do and so little time.

Karen pulled at the mass of yarn that she held in her lap and stared at the pale form of her sister. She found that she looked forward to awkward moments with her ex-husband. Compared to this . . .

And Karen sat and watched her sister die.

Chapter 25

Dear Diary,

I'm not exactly the sort to keep diaries. I've had dozens over the years, but I never really write in them every night. It always seems like there's something else to do by the time Day Seventeen rolls around. I think I still have about six half-started journals in the closet underneath the fondue pots. But Claire said this might be good for me so that I can remember what happened. "To remember is to learn," she says, although why everyone around me seems to be so bloody wise all of a sudden I've no idea. (I could use a little dose of it myself if you're listening up there.)

I meant what I said to Patrick. I can deal with it. I know so much more about myself after this past week. It sounds like some cheesy network television movie, but I really do feel alive after . . . anyway, I am getting ahead of myself . . . I guess I don't want to think about it.

But I have to.

I suppose I should just say what happened and get on with it, but putting it into words, actually writing it down, is harder than I thought. I've never been good at describing things, so I guess Mark was right too. I don't observe things. I want to get this right in every detail, but I don't really notice what the color of the drapes are, or the way wind blows across grass. Life just kind of flows over me most of the time. But I'll try, because there are times when I do notice things, a lot of things. This was one of them.

I had it with me. It was in my purse, of course, from Friday night. So much goes into my pocketbook and so little ever escapes again.

"I brought this for you."

I knew she couldn't hear me, but I said it anyway. I placed her arms across her chest and wrapped one of her hands around the picture and wrapped the other around my own.

"I know you can't see it, but I wanted you to have it. It helped me when things have gotten bad lately."

I watched the light gray mist creep across the clear plastic of her respirator, fascinated by the ebb and flow of her breaths. The lull seemed like forever between those waves of mist. I squeezed her hand tighter as I watched, so hard I could feel the individual bones of her fingers. I don't know what I was trying to do. Hold on as long as I could, I guess.

I've felt alone in my life, diary. More times in the past few years than I care to remember. It hurts. Like someone taking a blade and gouging out your insides, leaving an emptiness deep down within you. But you don't know it all the time: loneliness just picks its moment and slams into you like a freight train, showing you just exactly how alone you really are. I've had several of those moments. When Michael drove off that night. When Mom died. Too many.

This was the worst.

In that quiet, white, sterile hospital room that day I found myself weeping over the shade of my sister.

I wept trying to fill up the silence in the room. Inside me. "Tommy has a job offer with the Service," I blurted out.

I cleared my throat and rubbed my nose with my fist. The tears kept coming though.

I chuckled. Well, it was either that or a snort.

"Jim still doesn't know what he wants to do with his life," I barked, my laughter and crying mixing, becoming indiscernible sobs of sound. "Just like me."

I think I stuffed my fist in my mouth at that point. I just had so much to say, to explain the past ten years, but she knew it already and she couldn't hear but I just wanted to say, ". . . I don't know how you can ever forgive me . . . but . . . I love you."

It was then I felt the creased and flaky skin of her hand press back against my sweat-soaked palm.

Her eyelids fluttered open.

I found myself staring at those wonderful hazel eyes, clear and sharp.

Her mouth opened, thin lips cracking as her jaw worked up and down, trying to find a sound for her voice to form a soft whisper that would float over the linen and across the years.

But no sound came out.

The pain was too much.

Instead, she raised her hand and stroked my head.

I smiled at her. I must have looked hideous with snot running down my nose, and streams of tears running down the canals of the wrinkles of my face. I could have scared away a buffalo.

Beth smiled back.

I forgot how much I missed that smile.

Chapter 26

Dear Diary,

It's been a while since my last entry, apparently.

I told you I was horrible at this.

I'm in one of those Christmas Cozy Fireglow Moments, I guess. Minus the Fireglow. I think I just want to start a New Year fresh.

Elizabeth Lacey Whittington is home. Right now, she's tucked up in bed watching the Grinch on the old little portable, propped up on her pillows.

She's . . . She's not great. She has good days and bad days. But okay generally. And, to me, "okay" is fabulous. She wasn't in a coma or anything. That first time I saw her I was just so shocked at our—her condition.

Mr. Hobbes has become her biggest fan. Someone who can spend all day sleeping with him and petting him. He's even stopped leaving "presents" in Michael's sock drawer.

Yes, Diary, believe it or not Michael's around too. Well, mostly. He spends long periods of time gone on business, which is good, and when he's back, I move out to the guest house.

It's weird, but when I watch him look at her, I feel happy that they're happy.

I always thought I was more bitter than that.

Luke helps. We fight. A lot. Which I enjoy, for some reason.

We make up. A lot. Which I also enjoy. For more obvious reasons.

We have nothing in common. And it works. When he goes running by the river, I pick up the latest novel and read. I've also started a little Romance Reading group at the library once a month, to pick out the latest quality novels. We've even started writing to publishers, suggesting what we want to read. Luke used to make comments, but I told him to leave it be. It's my thing.

Once a month we go dancing at the "library social center." Mavis now runs the thing, so it gives her something to do. We still bicker, of course. I don't think I'm happy without a villain in my life, even if it is only an overweight library director. Emma's temporary work-visa has expired, so before she returned to England, we had a big send off on one of the dance nights.

Speaking of dancing, it turns out Luke and I are fantastic at it! (Thanks to some lessons from Mark, mind you). I'm not sure how long we will last as a couple—marriage is the FARTHEST thing from my mind for even more obvious reasons. But he makes me feel good. I hope I make him feel good too. Scares me a bit sometimes.

Not half as scary as when I discovered that Luke and Michael actually *like* each other. Bizarre.

We're all having supper together tonight and then Claire and Mark are coming over after for some drinks. Beth has been resting up for days so that she can sit with us at the table in her chair. Mr. Hobbes has been spastic all day throwing himself against the oven door—smelling a turkey roasting for four hours has that effect on him. Of course, Michael chucking a potato at poor Mr. Hobbes didn't help much. Luke's doing stuffing and Tommy is in charge of the can of cranberry sauce (tradition). I don't know how Tommy feels about Luke. Probably find out eventually . . . all that to look forward to, I guess. Tommy's in the Corps, bringing water to villagers somewhere in the Pacific. I sent him cookies. He said he hates it when I do that, but I know he really doesn't. Mothers know.

And I'm sitting by the Christmas tree, writing. I'm on the floor with my legs crossed and presents splayed around my feet. I love it. :)

A new year is coming. Feels really weird. I know the next few months probably won't be easy, the doctor's still say anything can happen, but . . . but . . . but what? I really don't know. I don't think this is a Happily Ever After scenario, more of a Moderately Content for Now motif.

That's for later. For now, I have a family again, if a slightly odd one. I've got an unemployed son calling his girlfriend long distance on the telephone, my ex-husband arguing with my boy(?)friend in the kitchen about carving knives, a spastic cat writhing in tinsel by my knee and my sister back where she belongs: at home.

Thank you, Santa. It was just what I asked for. Sort of.

And more.

Acknowledgements

I hope you enjoyed *Whisterpoop*. First and foremost, I would like to thank the librarians of the Potsdam Public Library. They were silly enough to employ me as a teenager and they helped shape my life. I am indebted to my parents, also librarians, for their continued support over the years. Being raised by librarians means that you always have plenty of books around and plenty of silence, which are both invaluable. Thanks are due to my cats over the years: Sassafrass, Hobo, and Kaylee.

Whisterpoop began life on a floppy disk twenty years ago, then surfed many different hard drives as I traveled around the world. While I lost many laptops over the years, I kept finding this story on backup drives, as if it was waiting patiently for the right time to be re-discovered. Now, in 2021, I would like to extend my thanks to Tiffany Manriquez for encouraging me to resurrect it. I would also like to thank the participants of San Diego State University's MFA program (2002), including the fantastic Joanne Meschery and Suzanne Deal, who helped me finish the story. Technically, *Whisterpoop* began in 1997 when I *should* have been writing my master's thesis on volcanology, but don't tell my thesis advisor.

If you enjoyed this story, please take a moment to leave a review on the site of your choice. Reviews make a huge difference to independent authors and will help me continue to write more novels.

Visit RJCorganbooks.com for more information.

About the Author

R. J. Corgan currently lives in Virginia with his partner, their dog Rocky, and their cat, Nikita. While trained as a geologist and cartographer, R. J. currently spends his days attending endless meetings, for reasons no one can adequately explain. He has worked on scientific expeditions in Iceland, Central America, and Africa. He has written three murder mysteries set in those locales: *Cold Flood, The Meerkat Murders*, and *Murder on Masaya*. The fourth book in the series, *Mammoth Drop*, will be released in 2022. *Whisterpoop* is his first romantic comedy.

Made in the USA
Coppell, TX
04 January 2022

70861203R00085